PALATINE PUBLIC LIBRARY

3 1265 01599 0429

S0-AGI-336

OFFICIALLY
WITHDRAWN

Jan 2018

AT THE RUTHLESS
BILLIONAIRE'S
COMMAND

AT THE RUTHLESS BILLIONAIRE'S COMMAND

BY

CAROLE MORTIMER

MILLS & BOON
BOON

PALATINE PUBLIC LIBRARY DISTRICT
700 N. NORTH COURT
PALATINE, ILLINOIS 60067-8159

All rights reserved including the right of reproduction in whole or in part in any form. This edition is published by arrangement with Harlequin Books S.A.

This is a work of fiction. Names, characters, places, locations and incidents are purely fictional and bear no relationship to any real life individuals, living or dead, or to any actual places, business establishments, locations, events or incidents. Any resemblance is entirely coincidental.

This book is sold subject to the condition that it shall not, by way of trade or otherwise, be lent, resold, hired out or otherwise circulated without the prior consent of the publisher in any form of binding or cover other than that in which it is published and without a similar condition including this condition being imposed on the subsequent purchaser.

® and TM are trademarks owned and used by the trademark owner and/or its licensee. Trademarks marked with ® are registered with the United Kingdom Patent Office and/or the Office for Harmonisation in the Internal Market and in other countries.

First published in Great Britain 2017
By Mills & Boon, an imprint of HarperCollins*Publishers*
1 London Bridge Street, London, SE1 9GF

Large Print edition 2018

© 2017 Carole Mortimer

ISBN: 978-0-263-07323-2

MIX
Paper from
responsible sources
FSC
www.fsc.org   FSC™ C007454

This book is produced from independently certified FSC™ paper to ensure responsible forest management. For more information visit www.harpercollins.co.uk/green.

Printed and bound in Great Britain
by CPI Group (UK) Ltd, Croydon, CR0 4YY

With many thanks to all
at Harlequin Mills & Boon

PROLOGUE

'WHAT'S *HE* DOING HERE?' Lia couldn't take her eyes off the man standing back slightly on the other side of the open grave where her father's coffin would soon be laid to rest.

'Who—? Oh, God, no…'

Lia ignored her friend's gasp of dismay as her feet seemed to move of their own volition, taking her towards the dark and dangerous man whose image had consumed her days and haunted her nightmares for the past two weeks.

'Lia—no!'

She was barely aware of shaking off Cathy's attempt to restrain her, her attention focused on only one thing. One man.

Gregorio de la Cruz.

Eldest of the three de la Cruz brothers, he was tall, at a couple of inches over six feet. His slightly overlong dark hair was obviously professionally styled. His complexion was olive-toned. And his face was as harshly handsome as that of a conquistador.

Lia knew he was also as cold and merciless as one.

He was the utterly ruthless, thirty-six-year-old billionaire CEO of the de la Cruz family's worldwide business empire. A business empire this man had carved out for himself and his two brothers over the past twelve years by sheer ruthless willpower alone.

And he was the man responsible for driving Lia's father to such a state of desperation that he'd suffered a fatal heart attack two weeks ago.

The man Lia now hated with every particle of her being.

'How dare you come here?'

Gregorio de la Cruz's head snapped up and he looked at Lia with hooded eyes as black and soulless as she knew his heart to be.

'Miss Fairbanks—'

'I asked how you *dare* show your face here?'

she hissed, hands clenched so tightly at her sides she could feel the sting of her nails cutting into the flesh of her palms.

'This is not the time—'

His only slightly accented words were cut off as one of Lia's hands swung up and made contact with the hardness of his chiselled cheek, leaving several smears of blood on his flesh from the small cuts in her palm.

'No!' He held up his hand to stop two dark-suited men who would have stepped forward in response to her attack. 'That is the second time you have slapped my face, Amelia. I will not allow it a third time.'

The second time?

Oh, goodness—yes. Her father had introduced them in a restaurant two months ago. They had both been dining with other people, but Lia had been totally aware of Gregorio de la Cruz's gaze on her, following that introduction. Even so, she had been surprised when she'd left the ladies' powder room partway through the evening to find him waiting for her outside in the hallway.

She had been even more surprised when he'd told her how much he wanted her before kissing her.

That was the reason she had slapped his face the first time.

She had been engaged at the time—he had been introduced to her fiancé as well as her that evening—so he had stepped way over the line.

'Your father would not have wanted this.' He kept his voice low, no doubt so none of the other mourners gathered about the graveside would be able to hear his response to her attack.

Lia's eyes flashed with anger. 'And how the hell would you know what my father would have wanted when you don't—*didn't*—know the first thing about him? Except, of course, that he's dead!' she added vehemently.

Gregorio knew far more about Jacob Fairbanks than his daughter obviously did. 'I repeat—this is not the time for this conversation. We will talk again once you are in a calmer state of mind.'

'Where you're concerned that's never going to happen,' she assured him, her voice harsh with contempt.

Gregorio bit back his reply, aware that Amelia Fairbanks's aggression came from the intensity of her understandable grief at the recent loss of her father—a man Gregorio had respected and liked, although he doubted Jacob's daughter would believe that.

The newspapers had featured several photographs of Amelia since the start of the worldwide media frenzy after her father had died so suddenly two weeks ago, but having already met her—*desired her*—Gregorio knew none of the images had done her justice.

Her shoulder-length hair wasn't simply red, but shot through with highlights of gold and cinnamon. Her eyes weren't pale and indistinct, but a deep intense grey, with a ring of black about the iris. She was understandably pale, but that pallor didn't detract from the striking effect of her high cheekbones or the smooth magnolia of her skin. Long dark lashes framed those mesmerising grey eyes. Her nose was small and pert, and the fullness of her lips was a perfect bow above a pointed and determined chin.

She was small of stature, her figure slender, and the black dress she was wearing seemed to hang a little too loosely—as if she had recently lost weight. Which he could see she had.

Nevertheless, Amelia Fairbanks was an extremely beautiful woman.

And the sharp stab of desire he felt merely from looking at her and breathing in the heady spice of her perfume was totally inappropriate, considering the occasion.

'We will talk again, Miss Fairbanks.' His tone brooked no argument this time.

'I don't think so,' she said, scorning his certainty.

Oh, they *would* meet again. Gregorio would ensure that they did.

His gaze was guarded as he gave her a formal bow before turning on his heel to walk across the grass and get into the back of the black limousine waiting for him just outside the graveyard.

'Señor de la Cruz?'

Gregorio looked up blankly at Silvio, one of

his two bodyguards, to see the other man holding out a handkerchief towards him.

'You have blood on your cheek. Hers, not your own,' Silvio explained economically as Gregorio gave him a questioning glance.

He took the handkerchief and rubbed it across his cheek before looking down at the blood that now stained the pristine white cotton.

Amelia Fairbanks's blood.

Gregorio distractedly put the bloodied handkerchief into the breast pocket of his jacket as he glanced across to where she stood beside a tall blonde woman at her father's graveside. Amelia looked very small and vulnerable, but her expression was nonetheless composed as she stepped forward to place a single red rose on top of the coffin.

Whether she wished it or not, he and Amelia Fairbanks would most definitely be meeting again.

Gregorio had wanted her for the past two months—he could wait a little longer before claiming her.

CHAPTER ONE

Two months later

'I NEVER REALISED I'd accumulated so much *stuff.*'

Lia groaned as she carried yet another huge cardboard box into her new apartment and placed it with the other dozen boxes stacked to one side of the tiny sitting room. The other half was full of furniture.

'I'm sure I don't need most of it. I definitely have no idea where I'm going to put it all.' She looked around the London apartment with its pocket-size sitting room/kitchen combined, one bedroom and one bathroom. It was a huge down-size from the three-storey Regency-style town-house she had shared with her father.

Beggars couldn't be choosers. Not that Lia was exactly a beggar—she had a little money of her own, left to her by the mother—but the comfortable lifestyle she'd known for all of her twenty-five years no longer existed.

Every one of her father's assets had been frozen until the extent of his debts had been decided and paid by his executors—which would take months, if not years. Considering the dire financial situation her father had been in before his death, Lia doubted there would be anything left.

Their family home had been one of those assets, and although Lia could have continued to live there until everything was settled she hadn't wanted to. Not without her father. The business sharks were also circling, ready to snap up the assets of Fairbanks Industries as soon as the executors had decided when and how they were going to be sold off to pay the debts.

Lia had used her own money to pay her father's funeral expenses and the deposit on this apartment, plus the few bits of furniture she had deemed necessary to fill the tiny space. She hadn't been allowed to remove anything from the house except personal items.

She had resigned from all the charitable work

that had taken up much of her time—with her father dead and his estate in limbo those charities no longer considered the name Fairbanks as being a boon to their cause!—and she'd looked for, and found, a job that paid actual wages. She needed to be able to earn enough at least to feed herself and continue paying the rent on this apartment.

She had taken charge of her own life, and it felt strangely good to have been able do so.

Cathy shrugged. 'You must have thought you needed it when you did the packing.'

She didn't add what both of them knew: a lot of the contents of these boxes weren't Lia's at all, but personal items of her father's she had packed and been allowed to bring from their home. Items that had no value but which had meant something to him, and which Lia couldn't bear to part with.

Lia had put all these boxes in storage for the past two months, while she'd stayed with her best friend Cathy and her husband Rick. That had been balm to her battered emotions, but a situation Lia had known couldn't continue indefinitely. Hence her move now to this apartment.

She was over the absolute and numbing shock of finding her father in his study, slumped over his desk, dead from a massive heart attack the paramedics had assured her would have killed him almost instantly. Cold comfort when they'd been talking about the man Lia had loved with her whole heart.

In some ways she wished that previous numbness was still there. The loss of her father's presence in her life never went away, of course, but now a deeper, more crippling agony at the loss would suddenly hit her when she least expected it. Standing in the queue at the local supermarket. Walking in the park. Lying in a scented bubble bath.

The loss would hit her with the force of a truck, totally debilitating her until the worst of the grief had passed.

'Time for a glass of wine, methinks,' Cathy announced cheerfully. 'Any idea which one of these boxes you put the wine glasses in?' The tall blonde grimaced at the stack of unopened boxes.

'I'm space-challenged—not stupid!' Lia grinned as she went straight to the box marked 'Glassware', easily ripping off the sealing tape to take out two newspaper-wrapped glasses. 'Ta-da!' She held them up triumphantly.

Lia had no idea what she would have done without Cathy and Rick after her father died. The two women had been friends since attending the same boarding school from the age of thirteen, and Cathy was as close to her as the sister she had never had. Closer, if what she'd heard about sisterly rivalry was true.

Luckily Cathy worked as an estate agent, and was responsible for helping Lia find this afford-able apartment. But, even so, there was only so much advantage she could take of Cathy's friend-ship.

'You should go home to your husband now,' she encouraged as the two of them sat on a couple of the boxes drinking their wine. 'Rick hasn't seen you all day.'

Rick Morton was one of the nicest men Lia had ever met—as much of a friend to her as Cathy was, especially this past two months. But the poor man must be longing to have his wife and his apartment to himself.

'Are you sure you're going to be okay?' Cathy frowned.

'Very,' Lia confirmed warmly.

Rick had been persuaded to go off and enjoy a football match with his friends that afternoon. A welcome break for him, it had also allowed the two women to move Lia into her new home. But there had to be a limit to how much and for how long Lia could intrude on the couple's marriage.

'I'm just going to unpack enough to be able to make the bed and cook myself something light to eat before I go to sleep.' Lia gave a tired yawn: it had been a long day. 'I don't just have a new apartment to organise, but a new job on Monday morning to prepare for too!'

Cathy slipped her arms into her jacket. 'You're going to do just fine.'

Lia knew that. After the past two months she

had no doubt that she was capable of looking after herself. Nevertheless, she still had to fight down the butterflies that attacked her stomach whenever she thought of all the changes in her life since her father had...*died*. She still choked over that word—probably because she still couldn't believe he was gone.

And he wouldn't be if Gregorio de la Cruz hadn't withdrawn De la Cruz Industries' offer to buy out Fairbanks Industries. The lawyers might have presented that death knell to her father, but there was no doubt in Lia's mind that it was Gregorio de la Cruz who was responsible for the withdrawal of that offer.

Her father had watched the decline of his company for months and, knowing he was on the edge of bankruptcy, had decided he had no choice but to sell. Lia firmly believed it was the withdrawal of the De la Cruz offer that had been the final straw that had broken him and caused her father's heart attack.

Which was why all of Lia's anger and resentment was now focused on the man she held responsible.

Futile emotions when there was no way she would ever be able to hurt a man as powerful as Gregorio de la Cruz. Not only was he as rich as Croesus, but he was coldly aloof and totally unreachable.

The man had even been accompanied by two bodyguards at her father's funeral, for goodness' sake. They hadn't been able to prevent Lia from slapping him, though. Was that because Gregorio de la Cruz had *allowed* it? He had certainly indicated that the two men should back off when they would have gone into protection mode.

She was thankful it had been a private funeral, and that there had been no photographs taken of the encounter to appear in the newspapers the following day and stir up the media frenzy once again. There'd been enough speculation after her father's sudden death without adding to it with her personal attack on Gregorio de la Cruz.

Nevertheless she had found a certain satisfaction in slapping the Spaniard's austerely handsome face. Even more so at seeing *her* blood streaked across his tautly clenched cheek.

As the days, weeks and then months had passed, and Gregorio de la Cruz's chilling promise that they would talk again hadn't come to fruition, Lia had mostly been able to put the man out of her mind. Just as well, because she only had enough mental energy to concentrate on the things that needed her immediate attention. Such as packing up the house, with Cathy and Rick's help, and finding herself an apartment and a job.

But she had successfully done all those things now—including securing a job as a receptionist in one of London's leading hotels.

Having no wish to start answering awkward questions from a prospective employer or, even worse, become the recipient of sympathetic glances that just made her want to sit down and cry, Lia had applied for several jobs under the name Faulkner—her mother's maiden name.

Nevertheless, she had no doubt it was her years of being *the* Amelia Fairbanks that had given her the necessary poise to secure her job. The manager of the hotel had obviously liked her appearance and manner enough to give her a one-day trial. He had admitted afterwards to being impressed with her warmth and the unflappable manner with which she'd dealt with some of their more difficult clientele.

The poor man had no idea she was usually on the other side of the reception desk, booking in to similar exclusive hotels all over the world.

So—new apartment, new job.

Cathy was right: she was going to be just fine.

But not if one of her new neighbours was going to ring her doorbell at nine o'clock at night, when she was soaking in a much-needed bath after having pushed herself to empty half a dozen of the boxes once she'd eaten a slice of toast.

It had to be one of her new neighbours, because Lia hadn't sent out new address cards to any of her friends yet. It was the next job she had to do—once she had unpacked completely and arranged her furniture ready for receiving visitors.

Not that she expected there to be too many of those. Amazing how many people she had thought were friends had turned out not to be so once she was no longer Amelia Fairbanks, daughter of wealthy businessman Jacob Fairbanks. Even David had broken their engagement.

But she refused to think about her ex-fiancé now!

Or ever again after the way David had deserted her when she'd needed him most.

Going to answer the door wrapped only in a bath towel was far from the ideal way to meet any of her new neighbours, but it would look even worse if Lia didn't bother to answer the door at all. It must be obvious she was in from the amount of noise she'd been making unpacking boxes and moving furniture around.

Impatient neighbours, Lia decided as the doorbell rang again before she'd even had chance to wrap the towel around herself.

She might be new to living in an apartment, but she knew at least to look through the peephole in the door before opening it. Except she couldn't see anyone in the hallway—which meant they had to be standing out of view. Well, there was always the safety chain to prevent anyone from coming in if she didn't want them to. And she *didn't* want them to. She was nowhere near ready—or dressed!—to receive visitors.

The reason her visitor had been standing out of the view of the peephole became obvious the moment Lia opened the door and saw Gregorio de la Cruz standing in the hallway!

'I do not think so.' He placed his handmade Italian black leather shoe in the six-inch gap left by the door chain, effectively preventing Lia from slamming the door in his face.

'What are you doing here?' Lia demanded, her hands gripping the door so tightly her knuckles showed white as she stared at the tall Spaniard.

He was once again dressed in one of those dark bespoke tailored suits, with a pristine white shirt and a perfectly knotted dark grey silk tie. Along with that slightly tousled hair, he looked like a catwalk model.

'You seem to have asked me questions similar to that several times now,' he answered evenly. 'Perhaps in future it might be wise of you to anticipate seeing me where and when you least expect to do so.'

Lia didn't want to *'anticipate'* seeing this man anywhere. Least of all outside the door to her apartment. An apartment he shouldn't even know about when she had only moved in today.

Except he was the powerful Gregorio de la Cruz, and he could do just about anything he wanted to do. Including, it seemed, finding out the address of Amelia Fairbanks's new apartment.

'Go to hell!' She attempted to close to door. Something that wasn't going to happen with that expensive leather shoe preventing her from doing so.

'What are you wearing? Or rather, not wearing...?'

Gregorio found himself totally distracted by the view he could see of Amelia's bare shoulders, where tiny droplets of water dampened her ivory skin, and what appeared to be a knee-length towel wrapped around the rest of her body. Her hair was loosely secured at her crown, with several loose tendrils curling against the slender-ness of her nape.

'None of your damned business!' There was a flush to her cheeks. 'Go away, Mr de la Cruz, before I call the police and ask them to forcibly remove you.'

He arched a dark brow. 'For what reason?'

'Stalking. Harassment. Don't worry, I'll think of something suitable by the time they get here,' she threatened.

'I am not worried,' he assured her calmly. 'I merely wish to speak with you.'

'You have nothing to say that I want to hear.' She glared at him, her eyes a deep metallic grey, the black rings wide about the irises.

'You cannot possibly know that.'

'Oh, but I do.'

Gregorio was not known for his patience, but he had waited for two long and tedious months be-fore seeking out this woman again. Two months during which he had hoped her emotions would not be quite so volatile. Obviously time had not lessened her resentment towards him. Or the blame she felt he deserved for her father's death at the age of only fifty-nine.

To say he had been shocked by Jacob Fairbanks's demise would be an understatement. Although it must have been a strain for the man—and his company—to have been under close scrutiny of the FSA financial regulators. They were still investigating, and all of Jacob Fairbanks's assets would remain frozen until their investigation was complete.

Gregorio had no doubt that it had been the withdrawal of De la Cruz Industries' offer to buy Fairbanks's company that had caused the FSA's investigation. But he would not be held responsible for the bad business decisions that had brought Jacob Fairbanks to the brink of bankruptcy. Or the man's fatal heart attack.

Except, it seemed, by Amelia Fairbanks...

'No bodyguards this evening?' she taunted. 'My, aren't you feeling brave? Facing a five-feet-two-inches-tall woman all on your own!'

Gregorio's mouth tightened at the jibe. 'Silvio and Raphael are waiting outside in the car.'

'Of course they are,' she scorned. 'Do you carry a panic button you can press, if necessary, and they'll come running?'

'You are being childish, Miss Fairbanks.'

'No, what I'm *being* is someone attempting to get rid of an unwanted visitor.' Her eyes flashed. 'Now, take your damned foot out of my doorway!'

His jaw tightened. 'We need to talk, Amelia.'

'No, we really don't. And Amelia was my grandmother,' she dismissed. 'My name is Lia. Not that I'm giving *you* permission to use it. Only my friends are allowed that privilege,' she added with a sneer.

Gregorio knew he was most certainly not one of those. And nor did *'Lia'* intend for him ever to become one.

It was unfortunate for her that Gregorio felt differently on the subject. He didn't only want to be Lia's friend, he had every intention of becoming her lover.

When his parents had died twelve years ago they had left their sons only a rundown vineyard in Spain. As the eldest of the three brothers, Gregorio had made it his priority to rebuild and expand, and now he and his brothers owned a vineyard to be proud of, as well as other businesses worldwide. He had done those things by single-mindedly knowing what he wanted and ensuring that he acquired it.

He had wanted Lia from the moment he'd first set eyes on her. He would not give up until he had her.

He almost smiled—but only almost—at the thought of her reaction if he were to state here and now that that was his intention. No, he knew to keep that to himself. For now.

'Nevertheless, the two of us need to talk. If you would care to open the door and put some clothes on…?'

'There are two things wrong with that demand.'

'It was a request—not a demand.'

She raised auburn brows. 'Coming from you, it was a demand. I don't *care* to open the door, *or* go and put some clothes on. And nor,' she continued when he would have spoken, 'as I've already said, do you have anything to say that I want to hear. Because of you my father is dead.' Tears glistened in those smoky grey eyes. 'Just leave, Mr de la Cruz, and take your guilty conscience with you.'

Gregorio's jaw clenched. 'I do not have a guilty conscience.'

'Silly me—of course you don't.' She eyed him scornfully. 'Men like you ruin people's lives every day, so what does it matter if a man had a heart attack and died because of you?'

'You are being melodramatic.'

'I'm stating the facts.'

'Men like me?' he queried softly.

'Rich and ruthless tyrants who trample over everyone and everything that gets in your way.'

'I was not always rich.'

'But you were always ruthless—still are!'

For the sake of his brothers and his own future, yes, he had become so. Had needed to be in a business world that would have eaten him up and spat him out again if not for that ruthlessness. But ruthless was the last thing he wanted to be where Lia was concerned.

He shook his head. 'You are not only being overly dramatic, but you are also totally incorrect in your accusations. In regard to your father or anyone else. As you would know if you would allow me to come in and talk to you.'

'Not going to happen.' She gave a firm shake of her head.

'I disagree.'

'Then be prepared to take the consequences.'

'Meaning?' Gregorio's lids narrowed.

'Meaning I'm being extremely restrained right now, but if you persist in this harassment I promise you I *will* take the appropriate legal steps to ensure you are made to stay away from me.'

He raised his brows. 'What legal steps?'

'A restraining order.'

Gregorio had never experienced this much frustrated anger with another person's stubbornness before. He was Gregorio de la Cruz, and for the past twelve years no one had dared to oppose him. Lia not only did so, but seemed to take delight in it.

He had never felt so much like strangling a woman and kissing her at the same time, either. 'Would you not have to engage the services of another lawyer in order to be able to do that?' he retaliated.

Colour blazed in her cheeks at his obvious reference to the fact that David Richardson was no longer her family lawyer *or* her fiancé.

'Bastard!'

Gregorio had regretted the taunt as soon as it had left his lips. At the same time as he couldn't take it back when he only spoke the truth. David Richardson had left this woman's life so fast after her father's death and Fairbanks Industries being put under investigation, Gregorio wouldn't be surprised if the other man hadn't suffered whiplash.

He took his wallet from the breast pocket of his jacket before removing a card from inside. 'This has my private cell phone number on it.' He held out the white gold-embossed business card to her. 'Call me when you are ready to hear what I have to say.'

Lia stared at the card as if it were a viper about to strike her. 'That would be *never*.'

'Take the card, Lia.'

'No.'

The Spaniard's jaw clenched as evidence of his frustration with her lack of co-operation. She doubted many people stood up to this arrogant man. He was far too accustomed to *telling* people what to do rather than asking.

Lia had acted as her father's hostess for years, so she had met high-powered, driven men like him before. Well...perhaps not *quite* like Gregorio de la Cruz, because he took arrogance to a whole new level. But she had met other men who believed no one should ever say no to them. Probably because no one ever had.

She had no problem whatsoever in saying no to Gregorio.

Lia didn't remember her mother, because she had died in a car crash when Lia had still been a baby. But for all Lia's life her father had been a constant—always there, always willing to listen and spend time with her. Their bond had been strong because of it. When her father had died Lia hadn't just lost her only parent but her best friend and confidante.

'I'm asking you to leave one last time, Mr de la Cruz.' She spoke flatly, sudden grief rolling over her, as heavy as it was exhausting.

Gregorio frowned at the way Lia's face had suddenly paled. 'Do you have anyone to take care of you?'

She blinked in an effort to ward off her exhaustion. Which in no way stopped her from continuing to fight him verbally. 'If I tell you that I'm alone are you going to offer to come in and make hot chocolate for me? Like my father did whenever I was worried or upset?'

'If that is what you wish.' He gave an abrupt inclination of his head.

'What I wish for I can't have,' she said dully.

Gregorio didn't need her to say that her wish was to have her father returned to her, because he could already see the truth of that in the devastation of her expression: the shadowed grey eyes, those pale cheeks, her lips trembling as she held back the tears.

'Is there anyone I can call to come and sit with you?'

'Such as…?'

Not her ex-fiancé, certainly. David Richardson could not have truly loved Lia, otherwise he would have remained at her side and helped her to weather the storm that had followed her father's death. Instead he had distanced himself from any scandal that might ensue once the investigation into Jacob Fairbanks's finances was complete.

Gregorio had no such qualms. He had no interest in the outcome of that investigation, nor in what other people might or might not choose to say about Lia or himself. His private life was most definitely off limits. He might not be in love with Lia but he certainly wanted her, and he would be pursuing that desire.

Lia appeared to be swaying now, and there was not a tinge of colour left in her face. She looked so fragile that a puff of wind might knock her off her bare feet.

What had she been doing when he'd arrived? She was obviously naked beneath the towel wrapped about her, but she claimed she was alone so she obviously wasn't entertaining a lover. The obvious explanation was that Lia had been taking a shower or a bath in order to wash away the dust of having moved in to her apartment today.

The loosely secured hair and the droplets of water that had now dried on the bareness of her shoulders would certainly seem to indicate as much.

'Take off the safety catch and let me in, Lia,' Gregorio instructed in his most dominating voice. It was a voice that defied anyone to disobey him.

She attempted a shake of her head, but even that looked as if it was too much effort. Her head seemed too heavy to be supported by the slenderness of her neck.

'I'm not sure I can,' she admitted weakly.

'Why not?'

'I... My fingers don't seem to be working.'

Gregorio stepped up close against the partially open door. 'Move your right hand slowly, then slide the catch along until it releases.' He held his breath as he waited to see if she would do as he asked.

'I don't want to.'

'But you will,' he encouraged firmly.

'I… It's… You…'

'Move your hand, Lia. That's it,' he encouraged gruffly as she hesitantly moved her hand towards the safety chain. 'Now, slide the lock along. Yes, just like that,' he approved softly. 'A little more—yes.'

Gregorio breathed softly as the safety chain fell free and he was able to push the door open. Not quickly or forcefully, but just enough to allow him to enter the apartment.

To be alone with Lia at last.

CHAPTER TWO

THE APARTMENT LOOKED to be in absolute chaos to Gregorio's gaze. There were boxes everywhere, and furniture stacked haphazardly in the tiny sitting room. The kitchen looked as if there had been an explosion of cooking utensils in its midst, and not a single surface was visible beneath pots and pans and cutlery.

Gregorio had never seen this side of moving to a new home before. The vineyard in Spain had belonged to his family for years, and the three de la Cruz brothers had grown up there. The rambling ranch-style house was full of family heirlooms as well as memories. And he had hired an interior designer to decorate and furnish the apartments he had acquired in New York and Hong Kong, as well as his houses in Paris and the Bahamas.

No wonder Lia was exhausted.

Lia managed to rouse herself slightly as she heard the finality of the closing of the door to her apartment. She wasn't completely sure how, but Gregorio de la Cruz was now standing inside her apartment, rather than outside in the hallway.

She remembered now… She had opened the door and let him in. Not because she'd wanted to but because she had felt *compelled* to. His voice, deep and mesmerising, had ordered her to un-latch the safety chain, and because she had been consumed by that black exhaustion she had done as he'd instructed.

He seemed taller and larger than ever in the confines of her untidy apartment. Taller, darker, and just plain dangerous. Like a huge jungle cat preparing to pounce on its unsuspecting prey.

The almost-black hair was in that tousled style again, and his face was set in harsh lines. His shoulders looked huge beneath the tailored suit, his chest defined and muscular, waist slender, hips and thighs powerfully muscular.

Lia could smell the aftershave he wore, easily recognising it as one that cost thousands of pounds an ounce. Even so there was a fine stubble on his chin, as if he was in need of his second shave of the day.

Her gaze moved quickly upwards and was instantly ensnared by glitteringly intense almost black eyes. 'I—'

'You need to sit down before you fall down.' Gregorio stepped across the room to remove several items from one of the armchairs before lightly grasping Lia's arm to support her until she was seated. 'Do you have any brandy?'

She somehow looked more fragile than ever seated in the chair.

'Wine,' she answered with a vague wave of her hand in the direction of the kitchen area.

Wine would not revive her as well as brandy, but it was still alcohol and better than nothing. Gregorio found a half full bottle of red wine on the breakfast bar, a used glass beside it. Predictably, it wasn't one of the de la Cruz vintages.

'Here.' Gregorio held the glass of wine in front of her until she took it from him with slender fingers that shook slightly. 'Have you eaten any-thing today?'

'Um…' Her forehead creased as she gave the matter some thought. 'A bowl of cereal this morn-ing and some toast this evening. I think…' she added doubtfully.

He scowled his displeasure before turning on his heel to stride through to the kitchen area. There was a loaf of bread on one of the units, a tub of butter and a carton of milk—and nothing else when he pulled open the fridge door and looked inside.

'You do not have any food.' He closed the fridge door in disgust.

'Maybe that's because I only moved in a few hours ago.'

Gregorio held back a smile at the return of her sarcasm. Evidence that Lia was feeling slightly better? He hoped so.

'Which begs the question—how did you know I'd moved in here today?' She eyed him suspi-ciously.

Gregorio had known about the apartment in the

same way he'd known about everything Lia had done in the two months since her father's death. He was given daily reports on her movements by his head of security.

No doubt it was an intrusion into her personal life that Lia would take exception to if she knew about it. But it was Gregorio's belief that the Fairbanks's situation was not yet over, and until it was she would accept his protection whether she wanted it or not.

'Drink your wine,' he ordered dryly as he took his cell phone from his pocket.

'Look, Mr de la Cruz—'

'Gregorio. Or Rio, if you prefer,' he added huskily. 'That is what my family and close friends call me.'

'Of which I'm neither. Nor do I intend to be,' she added dismissively. 'What are you doing...?' She frowned as he made a call.

'I had intended inviting you out to dinner, but now that I see how tired you are I am ordering dinner to be delivered to us here instead.' Gregorio put the cell phone to his ear, his gaze remaining challengingly on Lia as he waited for the call to be picked up.

Lia was starting to wonder if she had fallen asleep in the bath and was having another night-mare. Because Gregorio de la Cruz couldn't *really* be in her apartment, ordering dinner for both of them. Could he?

He certainly seemed real enough. Tall, muscular, and bossy as hell.

It seemed surreal after the months of torment she had just suffered through. Because of *him*.

Being a little unfair there, Lia, a little voice taunted inside her head.

Gregorio wasn't responsible for the decline of her father's company, nor the ailing economy. He had also been perfectly at liberty to withdraw his interest in buying Fairbanks Industries if he had decided the company wasn't viable.

Lia *did* believe it was the withdrawal of that offer which had resulted in her father's company being put under investigation, though, and only weeks later in her father's heart attack and pre-mature death.

She had to blame someone for all that, and Gregorio de la Cruz was the obvious person.

He had ended his call now, and was once again looking at her with those fiercely penetrating black eyes.

Lia's heart skipped a beat. Several beats. The blood rushed hotly through her veins as she saw something stirring in the cold depths of those dark orbs. Gregorio continued to stare at her. Something that looked like a flickering flame was growing stronger, hotter by the second, and was sucking all the air from the room as well as Lia's lungs.

She swallowed. Her heartbeat was now sounding very loud to her ears. So loud that surely Gregorio could hear it too? Lord, she hoped not! This man had kissed her once, and although Lia had slapped his face for it she had never forgotten it.

'I'm really not hungry.' She stood up to place the empty wine glass on the breakfast bar. Only to falter slightly as she realised how close to Gregorio she was now standing.

'I doubt you have felt hungry for some time

now,' he acknowledged softly. 'That does not mean your body does not need sustenance.'

Why did that sound so...so *intimate*—as if Gregorio wasn't talking about food at all?

Maybe because he wasn't?

Lia recognised the flame in his eyes for exactly what it was now. Desire. Hot, burning desire. *For her.* A desire he had demonstrated four months ago and which he obviously still felt.

She took a step back—only to have Gregorio take that same step forward, maintaining their close proximity.

She moistened her lips with the tip of her tongue. 'I think you should go now.'

'No.' He was standing so close his breath was a light caress across the soft tendrils of hair at her temples.

'You can't just say no.'

'Oh, but I can. I *have*,' he added with satisfaction.

Lia blinked up at him, her heart thumping wildly now, her palms feeling damp. 'This is insane.' *She* was insane. Because a part of her—

certain parts of her—was responding to the flickering flames in those coal-black eyes.

Her skin felt incredibly sensitised. Her nipples were tingling and between her thighs she was becoming slick with arousal.

'Is it?' Gregorio raised a hand and tucked a loose curl behind her ear before running his fingertips lightly down the heat of her cheek.

'Yes…' she breathed, even as she felt herself drawn to leaning into that caress.

Her father's death and David's defection meant it had been a long time since anyone had touched her, held her, apart from Cathy's brief reassuring hugs. Lia's body cried out for another kind of physical connection.

From Gregorio de la Cruz?

This man was a corporate shark who felt no compunction in gobbling up smaller fish. He was also a man who had a different woman on his arm in every news photograph Lia had ever seen of him. He bought and sold women—usually tall and leggy blonde women, who looked good on his arm and no doubt filled his bed at night—as easily as he bought and sold companies.

Lia wasn't tall, leggy or blonde.

Nor was she for sale.

She stepped back abruptly—only to give a shiver as she immediately felt the loss of the heat of Gregorio's body.

'I'm going to my bedroom to dress. I advise that you be gone by the time I come back.'

His sculpted lips curved into a smile. 'I make it a rule always to listen to advice, but I rarely choose to take it.'

Her chin rose challengingly. 'Is that because you're always right?'

His smile widened, revealing even white teeth. 'I have a feeling that however I answer that question you will choose to twist it to suit your own purposes.'

He was right, of course.

As always?

'Or should I say to suit the opinion you have formed of me without actually knowing me,' he added harshly.

Lia eyed him impatiently. 'I know enough to know I don't want you here.'

'And yet undoubtedly here I am,' he challenged.

'That's because you… Because I… You know what? Get the hell out of my apartment!' Her earlier agitation had returned, deeper than ever. 'Whatever sick game you're playing, I want no part of it.'

He sobered. 'I do not play games, Lia, sick or otherwise.'

'That's odd, because I'm pretty sure you're playing one now.'

Gregorio drew in a deep and controlling breath. Lia made no effort to hide her distrust and dislike of him. And right now her body couldn't hide her physical reaction to him.

Her breasts had plumped, her nipples hard as they pressed against the covering towel, and Gregorio's nostrils flared as they were assailed with the scent of her sweetly perfumed arousal.

Lia might distrust him, might think she had every reason to dislike him, but the response of her body told him she also desired him as much as he desired her.

He could wait to satisfy that desire. If he had to. And for the moment it seemed he must.

'I agree—you should go and put some clothes on.' He nodded abruptly. His self-control was legendary, but even *he* had his breaking point. And Lia, wearing only a towel to cover her nakedness, was it.

'Thanks so much, but I really don't need your permission to do anything!'

A nerve pulsed in his tightly clenched jaw. 'Dinner will be here shortly.'

'I've already told you I don't want any.'

Gregorio's eyes narrowed. 'Did your father have a line over which it was not safe to cross?'

'Oh, yes,' she recalled, with a wistful curve of her lips.

'And I am sure you knew to the nth degree how close to that line you might venture?'

'Yes...' She eyed him warily now.

'I have now reached my own line,' Gregorio informed her calmly.

'Is that supposed to scare me?'

Her bravado was admirable. Unfortunately it was nullified by the rapidly beating pulse visible in her throat: Lia was well aware of exactly how close she was to crossing over his line. And to paying the consequences for that trespass.

Gregorio's mouth thinned. 'You are—' He broke off as the doorbell rang. 'That will be Silvio, delivering our dinner.'

Her eyes widened. 'Wow, you must be a regular customer for the restaurant to have delivered so quickly.'

Their dinner had been prepared at and delivered by the staff at Mancini's, one of the most exclusive and prestigious restaurants in London. If Lia thought they were going to dine on pizza or Chinese food she was mistaken.

'Go and dress,' he instructed harshly. 'Unless you wish Silvio to see you wearing only a towel.'

Lia had a feeling the thought of that bothered Gregorio more than it bothered her. She was half inclined to remain exactly as she was—if only so that she could annoy Gregorio even more than he already was.

The fact that she knew she would feel more comfortable fully clothed was the deciding factor in her turning on her heel and walking down the hallway to her bedroom. But she was aware of Gregorio's devouring black gaze following her every step of the way.

Once in her bedroom, Lia slumped back against the closed door and drew in several deep breaths. Exactly what was going on here? Because something most certainly was.

Gregorio had not only kept the promise he'd made two months ago, that the two of them would talk again, but now that he was here in her apartment he was making no secret of the fact he still desired her.

Her body's traitorous response to him was harder for Lia to accept, let alone make sense of.

He was *Gregorio de la Cruz*, for goodness' sake. The man who'd had a hand in driving her father to his death.

When did I stop holding him completely responsible?

She hadn't. Had she...? No, of course she hadn't.

Gregorio was hard, ruthless, and scary as hell. He was also at least ten years older than she was, with the added experience that came with those extra years.

Dear God, she must be more desperate for human warmth than she'd realised if she'd been physically aroused by a man she should *hate*!

'Good?'

Lia's only response was a throaty 'mmm' as she dipped another piece of asparagus into melted butter before eating it with obvious enjoyment.

Gregorio had removed his suit jacket and tie, and rolled up the sleeves of his shirt to just beneath his elbows by the time Lia had returned fully dressed from her bedroom. Her hair was loose about her shoulders, in the style he preferred—but if Lia had known that he was sure she would have scraped it back into a severe bun!

She was wearing tight black jeans with a deep grey sweater that perfectly matched the colour of her eyes.

He had placed their food in the oven to keep warm, cleared the breakfast bar, found cutlery and laid two places so they were ready to eat as soon as Lia returned.

After stating that she wasn't hungry she had devoured succulent prawns and avocado with obvious relish, and steak, asparagus and dauphinoise potatoes were now being enjoyed with the same enthusiasm. The fact that she had drunk two glasses of the red wine Gregorio had ordered to be delivered with the meal—he'd had the foresight not to order one of the vintages from the de la Cruz vineyard—would seem to indicate she approved of that too.

Gregorio had found the food to be as delicious as always, but most of his enjoyment had come from watching Lia as she placed the food delicately in her mouth before eating with relish.

More colour returned to her cheeks the more she ate, and there was now a sparkle to her eyes.

Evidence that she really had been starving herself the past two months? Not deliberately, but because food had simply become unimportant to her with her life in such turmoil.

Gregorio intended to ensure that didn't happen again.

Lia was enjoying the food so much, and Gregorio seemed to be enjoying watching *her*, that there had been very little conversation between the two of them as they ate together.

Which was perhaps as well. Lia felt the need to argue with this man every time they engaged in conversation.

She finally placed her knife and fork down on her empty plate. 'I'd forgotten how much I enjoyed the food at Mancini's.'

Past tense, Gregorio recognised with a tightening of his mouth. Because Lia's world had been turned upside down and she could no longer afford to eat in such exclusive restaurants.

Which was his cue to resume their conversation about her father's death. A subject guaranteed to bring back the contention between the two of them, but also one that stood between them as an invisible barrier.

Gregorio would accept no barriers between himself and Lia—invisible or otherwise. He intended knowing everything there was to know about this woman. Inside as well as out. Intimately. And he intended her to know him in the same way.

'That was delicious. Thank you,' she added awkwardly. 'But it's been a long day, and now I think what I really need is to get some sleep.'

She did look tired, Gregorio acknowledged. Well-fed, but tired. And what did a delay of one more day or so matter when he had already waited this long for her?

He glanced at the disorder about them. 'Would you like me to come back tomorrow and help you with the rest of your unpacking?'

'Why are you being so nice to me?' Lia frowned her puzzlement, more confused than ever now that she had satisfied a need for food she hadn't realised was there until she'd begun eating.

Her stomach and her appetite had perked up at

the very first taste of the food from Mancini's—a restaurant she had enjoyed going to several times in the past, alone and with David or her father.

'You are a person it is easy to be nice to,' Gregorio dismissed with a shrug of his broad shoulders.

Shoulders that looked even wider and more muscular now that he was no longer wearing his jacket. In fact the whole casual thing he had going on—losing the jacket, taking off his tie, unfastening the top button of his shirt and rolling back the sleeves—had succeeded in making him more approachable and even more lethally attractive.

Which was perhaps his intention?

Lull the poor befuddled woman into a state of uncertainty and then pounce?

Cathy was never going to believe her when the two of them spoke on the phone tomorrow as they usually did, and Lia told her friend about Gregorio's visit and the fact the two of them had eaten dinner together.

Lia wasn't sure she believed it herself.

It was becoming more and more difficult to continue thinking of this man as the monster who had helped to destroy her father when he was being nothing but attentive and kind to her. No matter how rude she was, he continued to treat her with respect and kindness.

It's just his way of worming his way into my good graces before he goes for what he really wants!

Which Lia had now realised appeared to be *her*.

He was obviously a man who enjoyed a challenge if he thought he was going to win *that* battle.

'No, I'll be fine, thanks.' She stood up as indication that he should leave.

A hint he ignored as he remained seated at the breakfast bar. 'We have not eaten dessert yet.'

'Take it with you,' she dismissed. 'I couldn't eat another thing.'

'I could not deprive you of Mancini's celebrated chocolate cake.'

Lia gave a soft gasp. 'He really sent you some of his famous chocolate cake?' The dessert was

Mancini's secret recipe, and it had always been Lia's choice when she had dined at the restaurant. It was rich and decadent, and the taste of the cake was orgasmic.

'He sent *us* some of his chocolate cake,' Gregorio corrected.

'He didn't know I would be dining with you.'

'Oh, but he did. I spoke to Mancini personally and requested he send all your favourite foods.'

She widened her eyes. 'You *told* him we were having dinner together?'

Gregorio studied her from beneath hooded lids. 'Is there a problem with that?'

'Not for me, no.'

'Or for me.'

He certainly didn't *look* concerned at having announced to a third party that he was having dinner with the daughter of Jacob Fairbanks. Considering the speed with which some of her so-called friends and her fiancé had disappeared in a cloud of smoke, she found Gregorio's behaviour odd to say the least.

'You're a very strange man,' she said slowly.

'In a bad way or a good way?' he prompted as he stood up.

'I haven't decided yet.'

The grin he gave softened the harshness of his features. 'When you do, let me know, hmm?'

'You're different than I imagined.'

'In what way?'

'That night at the restaurant when you—when you kissed me, I thought you were just another arrogant jerk who doesn't like to hear the word no.'

'One out of the two, certainly,' he mused.

Lia didn't need him to tell her it was the word no he didn't like to hear. There was no doubting he was arrogant too, but there was something else. Something she couldn't quite equate with the ruthless bastard she'd labelled him. Perhaps it was the fact that, whatever his reasons, he was actually attempting to take care of her.

'You said you weren't always rich?'

'No.' He settled more comfortably on the bar stool. 'When I graduated from university with a business degree and returned to Spain it was to

find that my father had allowed the family vineyard to decline. Several years of bad harvest…
diseased vines.' He shrugged. 'There were still
my two brothers to go to university. I put my
own life on hold and set about ensuring that happened.'

'By founding the de la Cruz business empire?'

'Yes.'

'And is your life still on hold?'

He looked at her admiringly. 'Obviously not.'

Lia gave a shake of her head. 'I don't think it
would be a good idea for the two of us to meet
again.'

He looked displeased. 'Why not?'

Lia avoided meeting his gaze. 'Besides the obvious, I don't belong in that world any more.'

'The obvious…?'

'I hold you partly responsible for my father's
death.' There—she'd stated it clearly, so there
could be no lingering doubts as to her reason for
staying away from this man.

Was she protesting too much?

Because of her earlier reaction to him?

Maybe. But that didn't change the fact that she really didn't want to see or be alone with Gregorio again. He...unsettled her. Disturbed her. In a deep and visceral way Lia could never remember being aware of with any other man. Including the man she had once been engaged to and had intended to marry.

'I am sorry you feel that way,' he answered evenly. 'And you can belong in whatever world you choose to be in,' he announced arrogantly.

'You really can't be that naïve! My father is dead. My engagement is over. Most of my friends have deserted me. I've lost my home. My father's business is under investigation. None of the charities I worked for want the name Fairbanks associated with them. I now live in this tiny apartment, and I start a new job on Monday.'

'None of those things changes who *you* are fundamentally.'

'I no longer *know* who I am!' If there had been enough room to pace then Lia would have done so, as she was suddenly filled with restless energy. 'I try to tell myself none of those other things matter. That this is my life now...'

'But...?'

'But I'm mainly lying to myself.' She inwardly cursed herself as her voice broke emotionally. Gregorio was the last man she wanted to reveal any weakness to. 'And you're lying to *yourself* if you think that being nice to me, buying me dinner, will ever make me forget your part in what happened,' she added accusingly.

'No barrier is insurmountable if the two people involved do not wish it to be there.'

'But I *do* wish it to be there.'

'Are you sure about that?'

When had Gregorio moved to stand so close to her? She felt overwhelmed by both his size and the force of his personality—a lethal combination that caused her heart to start pounding loudly again.

'You have to go,' she told him.

'Do I?'

'Yes!'

Despite the food she'd eaten, Lia had no reserves of energy left to resist the pull of those dark and compelling eyes. No defences to fight the lure of that hard and muscular body. Even the reminder that he was Gregorio de la Cruz wasn't working. She was caught like a deer in the headlights of a car as his head slowly began to lower towards hers.

Gregorio was going to kiss her...

No matter how exhausted and defenceless Lia felt, she couldn't allow that to happen.

'No!' She raised enough energy to put a restraining hand against his chest, and that brief contact was enough to make her aware of the tensed heat of Gregorio's body and the rapid beat of his heart. 'You really do have to leave. *Please.*'

His lips remained only centimetres away from her own, his breath a warm caress against her cheek.

His nostrils flared as he breathed long and deeply before slowly straightening and then finally stepping away. 'Because you asked so nicely...'

Lia gave a choked laugh, able to breathe again

now that he was no longer standing quite so close to her. 'As opposed to threatening to call the police and having them kick you out?'

'Exactly.' He rolled down the sleeves of his shirt and fastened them before shrugging back into his jacket. 'Think of me tomorrow when you eat all that chocolate cake,' he added huskily, and then the door closed softly behind him as he let himself out of the apartment.

Lia breathed easily at last once he had gone. What the hell had happened just now? She had almost let Gregorio kiss her, for goodness' sake. She—

Lia froze as she saw the business card sitting on top of the breakfast bar.

The same business card she had refused to take from him earlier, with his personal mobile number embossed on it in gold.

CHAPTER THREE

'GOOD MORNING, LIA.'

Lia felt all the colour drain from her cheeks as she stared up at the man standing on the other side of the reception desk at the London Exemplar Hotel.

She had always thought that a person feeling the colour leeching from their face was a ridiculous concept: people couldn't actually *feel* the colour leaving their cheeks.

Except Lia just had. In fact the blood seemed to have drained from her head completely, settling somewhere in the region of her toes and leaving her feeling slightly light-headed as she continued to gape across the reception desk at Gregorio de la Cruz.

He tilted his head, a mocking smile playing about those sculpted lips as he saw her reaction to his being here. 'I did warn you that in future you should anticipate seeing me where and when you least expected to do so.'

Yes, he had—but it hadn't occurred to Lia that Gregorio might turn up at her new place of employment.

Deliberately so?

Or was it purely coincidence that Gregorio had come to the Exemplar Hotel on the morning she began working there?

Lia very much doubted that. With a man as powerful and well-connected as Gregorio there was no such thing as *coincidence*.

Which meant he had known she would be here. How he knew was probably by the same means he had acquired the address of her new apartment.

She narrowed her eyes. 'Are you having me followed, Mr de la Cruz?'

'Followed? No,' he dismissed. 'Am I ensuring your safety? Yes,' he admitted without apology.

Lia's brows rose. 'Why on earth does my safety need ensuring?'

'You are now alone in the world.'

'We both know why *that* is!'

'Lia—'

'Is there a problem here—? Mr de la Cruz!' Michael, the hotel manager, quickly hid his surprise as he greeted the other man warmly.

'Good morning, Michael,' Gregorio returned smoothly as the two men shook hands. 'And, no, there is no problem. I just came down to say hello to Miss… Faulkner,' he finished, with a knowing glance at the badge Lia had pinned on the left lapel of her jacket.

It was a surname Gregorio knew didn't belong to her.

And he also apparently knew the manager of this hotel by his first name'

An uneasy feeling began to churn in Lia's stomach, growing stronger by the second and making her feel slightly nauseous.

There was no such thing as coincidence where Gregorio de la Cruz was concerned.

Which meant he had known exactly where she would be starting her new job this morning.

He really was having her followed—might he even have had some influence in her attaining this job too?

For what reason?

The churning in Lia's stomach became a full-blown tsunami as she searched for the reason Gregorio was doing these things.

That guilty conscience she had accused him of having?

No, he had denied feeling any guilt in regard to her father's death.

The only other reason Lia could think of was to make her feel beholden to him. Not just beholden but trapped, when she badly needed to keep this job in order to pay her rent and bills as well as to buy food.

Trapped enough to give him what he wanted?

Namely herself.

'Of course.' Michael accepted Gregorio's explanation. 'If you would care to take your lunchbreak early, Lia, I'm sure we can accommodate—'

'*No!* No,' she repeated in a calmer voice as she realised how rude her previous vehemence must have sounded. 'I'm sure a busy man like Mr de la Cruz has somewhere else he needs to be right now.' Her eyes glittered in challenge.

Whatever was going on here, and whether or not Gregorio had had a hand in her acquiring this job, she did not want her co-workers seeing her on the receiving end of deferential treatment from the manager on her very first morning. There were already several curious glances being sent their way—goodness only knew what conclusions the people she had only just started working with were drawing about this conversation alone!

'Thank you for the offer, Michael.' Gregorio answered the other man smoothly. 'But, as Lia says, I have another appointment in a few minutes.'

'Oh. Okay. Fine.' The other man looked slightly flustered. 'I'll leave the two of you to talk, then.' He hurried off in the direction of his office behind the reception area.

'I do not like your hair pulled back in that style.'

Lia raised an irritated gaze. 'I really don't give a—'

'Language, Lia,' Gregorio drawled.

'*Down?*' she repeated abruptly. 'You told Michael you had come *down* to say hello to me...' she said as Gregorio raised a questioning brow.

'I occupy the whole of the penthouse floor of the hotel,' he admitted without apology.

Lia's heart sank down to wallow in all the blood that had already drained and congealed in her feet. 'Is it possible that you own the Exemplar Hotel?'

'It *is* part of the De la Cruz Hotel Group, yes.' He gave a smile of satisfaction.

Trapped!

Lia had absolutely no doubt now that for reasons of his own Gregorio was involved up to his arrogant neck in her being given this receptionist job.

Gregorio's satisfaction faded, his eyes narrowing as he recognised the flush gathering in Lia's cheeks for exactly what it was. Anger. White-hot burning fury.

'Do not do anything you will regret,' he warned softly as she stood up.

'The only thing I regret is actually thinking you

were being nice to me on Saturday.' She bent to retrieve her bag from under the desk, her eyes glittering accusingly as she glared across at him. 'I'm going to take that early lunchbreak, after all. Perhaps you would like to clear *that* with your buddy Michael?'

'He is not—'

'Stay away from me, Gregorio!' she hissed, leaning across the desk so that only he could hear. 'Find some other mouse to ensnare in your trap, but leave *me* alone!'

Her cheeks were ablaze with colour as she marched the length of the reception desk, appearing on the other side of it before striding the length of the hotel lobby and out through the front door.

Gregorio very much doubted it was the right time to tell Lia that the staff of the Exemplar Hotel were not allowed to use the front entrance.

Well, that hadn't gone as well as he might have hoped.

Hope.

That seemed to be all he had where Lia Fairbanks was concerned, when she continued to resist and deny him at every turn.

Maybe ensuring she was employed at one of the de la Cruz hotels hadn't been his best idea, but at the time, knowing of her lack of funds and the problems she was having finding suitable employment, it had seemed the right thing to do. Besides which, he knew Lia could do the job standing on her head.

She was warm, gracious, well-spoken, beautiful… And, having been her father's long-time hostess and companion, she knew exactly what was required of a receptionist in a prestigious hotel.

He should have waited until a more suitable time, of course, to inform her that he owned the hotel where she now worked. But, having spent a frustrating day yesterday, wondering what Lia was doing and who she was with, and knowing she was downstairs working in the lobby of the hotel, Gregorio hadn't been able to resist coming down at least to look her again.

Once he had seen her—as cool, calm and collected as he had known she would be—he hadn't been able to stop himself from actually speaking to her.

Considering Lia's fury when she left, he wasn't sure she would be coming back.

'So, how was your first morning at work?' Cathy prompted excitedly the moment she sat down at the table where the two women had arranged to meet for lunch. 'Met any gorgeous unmarried billionaires yet?' she teased as she made herself more comfortable by shrugging off her jacket.

Oh, yes, Lia *had* met an unmarried billionaire. But Gregorio de la Cruz's looks were compelling rather than pretty-boy gorgeous.

But he was a manipulator. He was having her followed. He had arranged for her to be employed at his hotel. He had literally taken away all her options. Until he owned her body and soul.

Body and soul?

Lia would be lying to herself if she didn't acknowledge her physical reaction to Gregorio. She only had to glance at him to be totally aware of him. Only had to look into those dark and compelling eyes to feel her body heating from the inside out.

Much as she might wish it wasn't true, she was physically attracted to Gregorio de la Cruz.

'Never mind,' Cathy sympathised, obviously misunderstanding the reason for Lia's silence. 'It was only your first morning, after all.'

For some reason, when the two women had spoken on the phone yesterday Lia hadn't told Cathy about Gregorio's visit to her apartment the evening before. Usually she told Cathy everything—had done since the two of them were at school together—but when it came to the subject of Gregorio, Lia didn't know quite what to say.

Maybe because yesterday she had still been a little uncertain in her conjecture as to the reason for Gregorio's visit the evening before—had still been wondering if perhaps she wasn't imagining things...desires...that simply hadn't been there.

On Saturday he had said he wanted to talk to her—which he hadn't. He had told her he would feed her dinner—which he had. And he had almost kissed her. He *would* have kissed her if Lia had allowed it.

His appearance at the hotel this morning—*the hotel he owned*—left her in no doubt that for reasons of his own Gregorio was weaving a spider's web about her. One made out of expensive dinners and the job she desperately needed, but still a spider's web.

Was he only doing these things because he *wanted* her?

Because he knew he couldn't have her any other way?

Lia found it hard to believe it was because Gregorio desired her. She had been complimented on the way she looked since men had first begun to take notice of her in her mid-teens. But she didn't fool herself into believing Gregorio was so bedazzled by her he would go to any lengths to have her. He only had to snap his fingers to have any woman he wanted, when he wanted her, so why bother even trying with a woman he knew had every reason to continue resisting him?

Maybe, despite his denials, he *did* feel some guilt in regard to her father's death?

'You okay, Lia?'

'Fine.' She determinedly shook herself out of her mood of despondency as she picked up the menu. 'Let's order, shall we?'

Until she knew what Gregorio was up to she had no intention of telling Cathy she had even seen him again, let alone that he was now pursuing her.

Relentlessly.

'Can I offer you a lift home?'

'No, thank you.'

Lia didn't need to look at the driver of the dark sports car driving slowly beside the pavement she was walking along to know it was Gregorio. Illegally kerb-crawling, of course—but then he seemed to be as cavalier towards the law as he was to everything else.

'You would prefer to take public transport rather than be driven home in the comfort of my car?'

'I would prefer to crawl home on my hands and knees than accept a lift from *you*!'

'You are being childish.'

'I am being the independent woman I now am—despite your efforts to make me otherwise!' Lia's hands clenched as she turned to glare through the open passenger window at Gregorio.

She had half expected to see him at the hotel again when she'd returned from lunch, and had breathed a sigh of relief when the afternoon had passed by without any more unwelcome interruptions from him.

She should have known he wouldn't give up that easily.

The car came to a stop and she stepped forward to bend down and talk to him directly through the open window. 'I realise you're a man accustomed to taking what he wants, and to hell with anyone else's feelings, but let me assure you I can't be bought or seduced into your bed with a few expensive dinners and a job— What are you doing?' she gasped as Gregorio turned off the car's engine before opening his door and climbing out of the low-slung vehicle.

His expression was dark and thunderous as he strode round the back of the car towards her. Lia instinctively took a step back.

He was dressed less formally than Lia had ever seen him before, in a black polo shirt open at the throat and worn beneath a soft black leather jacket, with jeans resting low down on his hips. The former emphasised the broadness of his shoulders and toned chest and abs, and the latter added to that rugged attraction. Gregorio looked breathtaking in a formal suit, but in casual clothes he was even more dark and dangerous.

Gregorio took a tight grasp of her arm as he opened the passenger door of the car. 'Get in,' he bit out between gritted teeth.

'I—'

'Get in the damned car, Lia, before I pick you up and put you there.' His voice was low and controlled. As if he might start shouting if he allowed himself to speak any louder.

It made Lia even more reluctant to put herself

in the vulnerable position of being alone in his car with him. At least out here in the street she had somewhere to run.

She raised her chin challengingly. 'I believe you are stepping way over *my* line now.' She reminded him of their conversation on Saturday.

Those black eyes glittered dangerously. 'You just made an outrageous accusation. One I do not intend to dignify with an answer when we are standing out here in the street, where anyone might overhear our conversation.'

Her cheeks warmed. 'You made the purpose of your interest in me obvious on Saturday evening. Or am I wrong in thinking you want me in your bed?'

A nerve pulsed in his clenched jaw. 'No, you are not wrong.'

She nodded. 'Which is why, after discovering you're now my employer, I have come to the conclusion I have.'

Gregorio never lost control. *Never.* He considered it a weakness to do so. And weakness could be exploited…manipulated.

Nevertheless, he knew he was seriously in danger of losing control at this moment. No one had ever accused him of the things Lia just had. No one would ever *dare*. No matter what she believed, he had no reason to manipulate her into an intimate relationship with him.

Not when he knew she felt the same desire for him that he felt for her...

Even if it *was* a desire she obviously didn't want to feel.

Gregorio's only motive in protecting and helping her was the fact that she no longer had anyone else in her life who would do so. The wealth she had grown up with and no doubt taken for granted was no longer there as a buffer either.

So, yes, Gregorio might have put in a word with Michael Harrington regarding employing Lia at the hotel, but his only reason for doing so had been an effort to give her back some of what she had lost.

For Lia to have reached the conclusion she had, that he was blackmailing her into a relationship with him as a result of his actions, was unacceptable. An insult of a kind Gregorio had never faced before.

The nerve in his jaw throbbed. 'We are having dinner together.'

'Did you not hear what I just said?'

'Of course I heard you,' Gregorio snapped. 'How could I do otherwise? But, as *I* said, I will not answer any of your accusations on a public street.'

His bodyguards had parked their SUV behind his sports car and the two men were now standing on the pavement a short distance away, watchful and alert to any and all danger.

'I have no intention of being alone with you. Anywhere,' Lia added with finality.

Gregorio stilled to regard her through narrowed lids. That last remark had been made so vehemently…

Lia's eyes were glittering brightly, her cheeks flushed and her lips full and pink. The evening was warm, and she had removed the jacket of her business suit as soon as she'd left the hotel. The cream blouse beneath was so sheer Gregorio could see the outline of her light-coloured bra. Her breasts were quickly rising and falling as she breathed deeply, the plumpness of her engorged nipples showed as a darker pink through the lace of her bra.

Gregorio slowly moved his gaze back up to her face. 'You want me too,' he stated.

'That's a lie!' Lia recoiled as if Gregorio had struck her, pulling her arm from his grasp as she did so. 'How could I possibly want you?' Her breathing became even more erratic. 'When you're the callous man who helped hound my father to his death?'

Lia heard herself say the words, saw Gregorio's reaction to them—his expression hardened and his eyes were once again those fathomless black pits—and all the time knew Gregorio was right. That she'd spoken so vehemently because she *did* want him. And she shouldn't. For all the reasons she had just stated.

Except her traitorous body was refusing to listen to her. Her breasts felt fuller and more sensitive and she felt the ache of arousal between her thighs.

'You are lying to yourself, Lia,' Gregorio dismissed scornfully. 'We both know that.'

'Your arrogance is only exceeded by your conceit!'

He gave a hard smile. 'When you are ready to hear the truth about your father I suggest you give me a call. Until then...' He turned to nod at the two bodyguards, indicating his intention of leaving.

'The truth about my father?' This time Lia was the one to place a restraining hand on Gregorio's arm, able to feel his tension through the soft material of his jacket. 'What are you talking about?'

He looked at her between narrowed lids. 'As I said, call me when you are ready to listen.'

'And my job...?'

He drew himself up to his full height, a couple of inches over six feet. 'Your continued employment is not conditional upon you agreeing to see me or listen to me. Or anything else.' His mouth was a thin line.

Lia's hand slowly dropped back to her side. 'I don't understand you...'

'Perhaps that is because—as you admitted the other evening—having now spoken with me, you find I do not fit with the preconceived prejudice you felt towards me?' he taunted.

There was some truth in that. No, there was a *lot* of truth in that, Lia conceded heavily. Gregorio was arrogant, and used to having—taking—whatever he wanted. But equally there had been no doubting his anger when Lia had made her accusations about his manipulating and trying to force her into a relationship with him.

He had also been considerate and unthreatening at her apartment on Saturday evening. If he really was as ruthless as Lia had thought him to be, then surely he would have forced the issue of wanting her then? He wouldn't have taken no for an answer when there had been a convenient bedroom just down the hallway.

After all, *she* might not have been aware of it at the time, but Gregorio had already known he held all the power.

And now he had implied that he knew something about her father that she didn't.

Lia gave a slight nod as she came to a decision. 'I'll have dinner with you in exchange for you telling me what it is you think you know about my father that I don't.'

She held her breath as she waited for Gregorio's response.

CHAPTER FOUR

'I THOUGHT WE would be having dinner in a restaurant.' Lia looked dazedly around the interior of the luxurious de la Cruz jet she and Gregorio were now seated on, being flown off to goodness knew where after boarding the jet at a private airfield fifteen minutes ago. 'I don't have my passport with me.'

'We are not going to land anywhere,' Gregorio assured her. 'And we do not need to go to a restaurant when I have persuaded Mancini to join us on board for the evening.'

If Lia had needed any convincing that Gregorio was super-rich—up there in the stratosphere wealthy—then the private jet and exclusive services of the chef were proof enough.

Except she hadn't needed any further proof of this man's wealth and power.

'We're just going to fly around while we eat our meal?'

'Why not?' He shrugged. 'It ensures our privacy.'

Privacy was the last thing Lia wanted with this particular man. A man she knew was starting to get to her, in spite of herself.

Gregorio knew the information he had about Lia's father was her only reason for allowing him to take her to dinner. Unfortunately his self-control was currently balanced on a very fine edge where Lia was concerned.

She hurled her insults at him as barbs meant to wound. They had succeeded in doing that, but her open defiance of him had also deepened the desire Gregorio felt to make love with her. To be consumed by the fire that burned between them whenever they were alone together. He wanted to strip every item of clothing from her body and gorge himself on her succulent flesh before burning in those flames.

'*Now* will you tell me what you think you know about my father that I don't?'

His gaze became guarded. 'Our agreement was that we would have dinner first.'

She gave a frustrated sigh. 'In that case we might as well eat.'

'So gracious,' Gregorio drawled as he stood up to remove his jacket.

A delicate blush coloured her cheeks. 'Why don't you just open and pour the wine?' she instructed him abruptly.

'Do you like to take charge in bed too?'

'Gregorio!' She gasped.

He raised speculative brows as he opened the white wine cooling in the galley, revealing none of the pleasure he felt at hearing her use his given name for the first time. 'I wasn't complaining. I merely wish to be pre-warned if that is the case.'

She looked more flustered than ever. 'I didn't accept your invitation—I'm only here because you promised to give me information about my father,' she reminded him flatly.

'All the while knowing how much I want you.'

'I was only— I didn't— Why do you always have to turn everything back to—?'

'My wanting you?' Gregorio finished softly. 'Perhaps because possessing you has obsessed my mind for some time now.'

She snorted. 'I find that very hard to believe!'

He poured the wine into two glasses before pushing one towards her, an indication that she should drink some of it. 'That I want you? Or that I have thought of you constantly since I first saw you?'

'I was engaged to another man!'

Gregorio gave a brief glance at her bare left hand. 'An engagement is not a marriage.'

'Obviously not,' she acknowledged heavily. 'But I find it difficult to believe you felt an instant attraction to a woman you had only just met.'

'Possibly because you prefer to continue believing me a man capable of *hounding* people to their deaths.'

She winced at this reminder of her earlier accusations. 'Talking of *possessing* someone—me—isn't exactly normal behaviour,' she defended.

'You would prefer that I flatter and seduce you with words before I attempt to make love to you?'

'That's the way it's usually done, yes.'

He gave a dismissive shake of his head. 'I have no time for such games.'

'And, personally, I would prefer it if you never referred to the subject again.'

'Then you are lying to yourself.'

'You—'

'Would you like me to show you how much you are lying?'

'No!' Lia could see the raw passion burning in his dark gaze.

He drew in a deep breath as he continued to study her for several long seconds. 'Drink some of your wine,' he finally encouraged huskily.

'And you call *me* bossy!' She eyed him impatiently.

He studied her over the rim of his glass as he took a sip of what proved to be a very good glass of white wine. He waited until Mancini had served their first course before speaking again. 'You believe me to be a male chauvinist?'

She grimaced. 'Maybe it's just a cultural difference?'

'You do not believe that any more than I do,' he observed dryly. 'And you should have met my father—compared to him I am a fully enlightened man who believes in equal opportunity for all three sexes.'

'He's…no longer with you?'

'Neither of my parents is still alive.' Gregorio inwardly berated himself for unthinkingly introducing the painful subject of the death of a parent. 'My father believed it was my mother's role to be a wife to him and to bring up their three sons.'

'And you don't?'

Lia took her glass of wine. Their conversation was far too personal for her liking. Combining that with how casually dressed Gregorio was this evening, this situation—the private jet, the personal chef—was all too disturbing for her peace of mind.

'My mother ensured my two brothers and I have

a more modern attitude.' Gregorio shrugged. 'For instance, she insisted all of us learn how to cook.'

'How did your father react to that?'

'As a man who had never had to learn how to so much as boil an egg, he was horrified,' Gregorio recalled with one of those smiles that changed his face from austerely attractive to devastatingly handsome. 'My mother loved my father enough to allow him to believe he was the patriarch of the family, when in actual fact she was the one who decided what, when, where and how.'

'She sounds amazing.'

Gregorio heard the wistful note in her voice—a reminder that Lia had grown up without a mother. It seemed as if every subject they touched upon had the potential to blow up in his face.

'She was,' he dismissed briskly.

'But you've never married?'

'There has been no time for a woman in my life.'

'That isn't what the newspapers say!'

'I was referring to a woman I might wish to marry.'

'Rather than go to bed with?'

His jaw tightened. 'Yes.'

'What happened to the woman you were having dinner with that night at the restaurant?'

'*Happened* to her…?'

Lia nodded. 'She looked nice.'

Gregorio's company had been in negotiations to buy Fairbanks Industries for some weeks before he had recognised Jacob Fairbanks in the restaurant that evening. Both of them had been dining with other people. David Richardson was known to him as Fairbanks's lawyer. But he'd never before met the woman seated between the two men.

She had been exquisite.

Gregorio had seen his dining companion seated before immediately going over to Fairbanks's table to seek an introduction to the beautiful redhead. Amelia Fairbanks—Jacob's daughter. And the lawyer was her fiancé.

When Amelia had stood up to go to the powder room half an hour later, Gregorio hadn't been able to resist following her. Or kissing her. Only to receive an angry slap to his cheek as soon as the kiss had ended.

The evening hadn't gone at all as Gregorio had originally intended it should. Not only had he mainly ignored his dining companion for the rest of the evening, in favour of staring at Amelia Fairbanks, but he had also put the other woman in a taxi as soon as they'd left the restaurant, rather than accepting her invitation to go back to her apartment for the night.

He straightened. 'I never saw her again after that evening.' Nor had he dated any other women in the past few months.

'Why not?'

He gave her a pointed glance. 'Because I saw you that night and I wanted you.'

Lia turned away from the intensity of that dark gaze. 'I can't imagine you allowing anyone— least of all me—to disrupt a single part of your life.'

'Can't you?'

She was so aware of everything about this man she was finding it hard to maintain the distance necessary if she was going to continue resisting him. Even more so after those revelations about his parents and his childhood. She didn't *want* to know things about Gregorio's life, to think of him as having been a child with loving parents and two younger brothers he had no doubt argued and fought with but would likely defend to the death if one of them was in danger. Knowing those things made him more a flesh-and-blood man and less the ruthless monster, Gregorio de la Cruz. Which had no doubt been his intention all along.

She must never forget who or what he was. Nor that he had revealed himself as someone who was not averse to using manipulation and machination to get what he wanted. And there could be no doubt now that he wanted *her*.

She glared at him. 'I'm not interested.'

'No?'

'No,' she snapped, seeing his knowing expression. But she knew he was right; she could never remember being this aware of a man before. Ever.

She had known David for over a year before

he'd asked her out and she'd accepted. They had dated for another year before he proposed and she had accepted. They had been engaged for just over a month before David had invited her back to spend the night at his apartment, and again she had accepted.

Up until the night David had ended their engagement he had been every inch the gentleman throughout the whole of their courtship.

Gregorio wasn't a gentlemen, and nor did he ever *ask* for anything he wanted. He just assumed it was his right and took it.

But wasn't it better that way?

To be simply swept off one's feet and not have to think about whether or not it was sensible, or consider the possible repercussions—?

No, of course it wasn't! Now that Lia was completely on her own it was even more important for her to be on her guard. Most especially so with Gregorio de la Cruz.

'You cheated,' Lia complained two hours later as she let the two of them into her apartment.

'I merely suggested we bring dessert back here.' Gregorio followed her inside.

'And so delayed answering my questions for even longer. Well, don't make yourself too comfortable,' she warned as Gregorio sat down at the breakfast bar. 'Because you aren't staying.'

'You *are* bossy in bed,' he said knowingly.

'You'll never know,' she assured him tersely.

Gregorio made no reply. Why bother contradicting her when it would only lead to another disagreement? When he was fully aware that Lia, in spite of herself, wanted him as much as he wanted her.

Besides, he could afford to concede a single battle when he had no intention of losing the war.

'Do you *want* any dessert?'

'I couldn't eat another thing after that delicious meal.'

'That's what I thought.' She put the dessert in the fridge before straightening. 'I've had dinner with you, fulfilled my part of the agreement, now it's time for you to start talking.'

She leaned back against one of the kitchen

cupboards, arms crossed defensively in front of her chest.

'Of course.'

Gregorio stood up in what was now a very tidy apartment. All the boxes had been emptied and removed, the furniture was neatly arranged, and several photographs of Lia and her father had been placed in prominent places.

'I liked your father very much—but obviously you choose not to believe that,' he said impatiently, acknowledging her sceptical snort.

'I have no reason to believe anything you say.'

'And *I* have no reason to lie to you.' He scowled. 'Lia, De la Cruz Industries did *not* withdraw from the negotiations to purchase your father's company.'

'Of course you did—'

'No,' he stated evenly. 'Your father was the one who withdrew from our offer.'

'That's ridiculous.' Lia pushed away from the kitchen unit, her movements restless as she walked into the larger area of the sitting room. 'Why on earth would he do that when he was on the verge of bankruptcy and so badly needed to sell Fairbanks Industries?'

'In light of the current FSA investigation into the company, I think we may assume it was because he had discovered some…discrepancy.'

'What sort of discrepancy?'

'I believe several million pounds were transferred from the company accounts to offshore bank accounts.'

'You *believe* or you *know*?'

'I know,' he confirmed quietly.

'My father did *not* steal from his own company, if that's what you're implying!' Her hands were clenched at her sides.

'Of course not.'

'Then who did?'

Gregorio shrugged his shoulders. 'Only a limited number of people had the means, and access to the bank accounts affected.'

She frowned as she thought over what Gregorio had told her.

He'd said her father had withdrawn from the negotiations to sell Fairbanks Industries. That he had done so because he had discovered someone had been stealing from his company.

But who?

As Gregorio had said, only a few people had access to the company bank accounts.

Her father, obviously.

And Lia, as a precaution—in case anything should ever happen to him and she needed access, he'd explained. How ironic that was, in the circumstances.

The two vice presidents of the company...

The accounts department only had limited access—not enough to be able to transfer funds from company accounts to another one.

There was no one else except—

Lia gave Gregorio a startled glance. 'Do you happen to know who he suspected?'

'I think you have already guessed the answer to that question.'

There was only one answer, if she eliminated everyone else. But it simply wasn't an answer Lia could give any credence to.

David had not only been her father's lawyer but

her fiancé when the embezzlement had supposedly taken place. Besides which, his family was incredibly wealthy. There was no incentive for David to steal money from her father's company.

Lord knew she had no reason to think kindly of David, after he had let her down so badly, but she simply couldn't believe the man she had intended to marry was capable of the things Gregorio had just revealed to her.

CHAPTER FIVE

'YOU'RE WRONG.' SHE gave a firm shake of her head.

Gregorio had watched the play of emotions on Lia's face. Puzzlement. Dawning realisation. Shock. Doubt. Followed seconds later by this out-right denial.

'Are you saying that because you *know* I'm wrong or because you hope that I am…?'

She looked at him blankly for several seconds. 'I'll admit David ultimately proved not to be the man I thought he was when I agreed to marry him, but he isn't the thief you're implying he is either.'

'Again, I ask—is that because you know for certain I'm wrong or because you don't want to believe I'm right?'

She straightened her shoulders defensively.

'David comes from a wealthy family. He's a partner in one of the most prestigious law firms in London. His father *owns* that law firm, for goodness' sake.'

'And you consider that proof of his innocence?'

'Well. No. Of course it isn't proof.' She shot Gregorio an impatient glance. 'But there is absolutely no reason why he would have stolen from my father.' Her chin rose in stubborn denial. 'David is a wealthy man in his own right.'

'My sources tell me that Richardson has a serious gambling habit.'

'Then *your sources* are wrong.' She gave a disgusted shake of her head. 'I went out with David for a year, was engaged to him for three months. David doesn't gamble.'

'I'm afraid he does. Excessively so. I am reliably informed that he lost over sixty thousand pounds in one casino alone last month.'

She gave a pained frown. 'But I never saw… There was never any hint… Can I really have been so wrong about him?'

Gregorio had known this was going to be a difficult conversation, and that was the reason he had delayed having it for as long as he could. He had known Lia would have a problem believing her ex-fiancé was guilty of theft on a grand scale, despite the other man having deserted her when she'd needed him. It was for this reason that Gregorio had been skirting around the edges of the subject for the past three days. He had known that once his suspicion was out in the open he would have no way of retracting it. That Lia would hate him all the more because of it.

Gregorio had no doubt the FSA would eventually find the missing funds, and the offshore bank account, but that would be the end of their investigation. They would have absolutely no jurisdiction in another country.

Gregorio wasn't hampered by such legalities. His own security people were even now following the money trail to the offshore bank account in the name of Madras Enterprises. He had no doubt they would eventually unravel the maze surrounding this mysterious company, and when they did Gregorio was sure they would be able to identify the owner of that company as being David Richardson.

If Richardson *was* involved, then he had probably considered it prudent to distance himself from the Fairbanks family after Jacob's death—starting with breaking his engagement to Lia. There was also the fact Lia was no longer wealthy, and Richardson was going to need a *very* wealthy wife with his obsessive gambling habit to satisfy.

'If— Whoever is responsible… My father *died* because of the strain he was put under!' Tears glistened in her eyes.

Gregorio's mouth thinned. 'I will get to the bottom of who is responsible, Lia, this I promise you,' he assured her grimly. 'And when I do they will be made to pay for what they did.'

'It won't bring my father back.'

'No.' What else could he say to a statement like that?

She dropped down into one of the armchairs. 'Then it really doesn't matter who's to blame, does it?'

She leaned her head back, closed her eyes.

It mattered to Gregorio. If David Richardson was responsible for the embezzlement then he couldn't be allowed to get away with what he'd done to the Fairbanks family. Nor could he be left in a position of power where he could do the same thing to other clients who put their trust him as their lawyer.

'Did you tell me these things so that I won't hate you any more?'

Gregorio's eyes narrowed as he looked across to see Lia now watching him guardedly. He could read nothing from her expression.

'I told you so that you would know the truth,' he said cautiously.

'But also so that I don't hate you any more?'

'Is this a trick question?' He eyed her warily. 'Do I damn myself whichever way I answer it?'

'Probably.' She gave a humourless smile as she stood. 'I think you should leave now. My head is buzzing with all that you've just told me, and I need to get my things ready for work in the morning.'

His gaze became searching. 'Are you going to be okay?'

'Yes.'

Lia wished she felt as positive as she sounded. The things Gregorio had told her tonight were disturbing, to say the least. She still didn't believe David was involved, but if her father really *had* discovered that someone was embezzling funds from Fairbanks Industries, and had withdrawn from the de la Cruz offer because of it, then she very much doubted that both men could be wrong in their suspicions.

She had only just started to put her life back together, and now she felt exposed and vulnerable again.

Moving in to her apartment and starting a new job had been positive things. A fresh start. Moving forward after weeks of feeling as if she were stuck in a quagmire of emotions with no way out.

Gregorio had given her a lot of information to think about tonight. Information about David that, if true, meant he was responsible to driving her father to his death. It also seriously brought into question the reason he had pursued her and asked her to marry him.

And her own ability to know if a person was trustworthy or not.

She had trusted David, and even if it turned out that he was innocent of Gregorio's accusations, David had still let her down by leaving her to deal with her father's death alone.

She had distrusted Gregorio the first timeshe met him, and yet he had done nothing but try to help her. Albeit for reasons of his own, he had apparently been protecting her this whole time—had been instrumental, she was sure, in helping her to acquire her job. By doing that he had given her back some of the pride and confidence in herself she had lost.

Was it possible that the good guy was really the bad guy and the bad guy was really the good guy?

Lia was giving herself a headache, trying to make sense of it.

'I'll walk you to the door,' she offered distractedly.

Gregorio knew he had no choice but to accept

that it was time for him to leave and he slowly followed Lia down the hallway to the apartment door.

Lia had a lot of new information to think about. But he didn't doubt for a moment that David Richardson was involved in this up to his pretty-boy handsome neck.

'Thank you.'

Gregorio blinked as he focused on Lia standing hesitantly beside the still closed door to her apartment. 'Sorry?'

She lifted her chin. 'I appreciate it must have been difficult for you to tell me those things.'

Gregorio drew in a slow and steadying breath, aware that Lia was placing a tentative trust in him.

'That doesn't mean I forgive you.' Her eyes narrowed. 'Only that for the moment I'm cautiously giving you the benefit of the doubt.'

He couldn't help but smile at her begrudging trust. 'I can live with that.'

'And call off whoever you have following me,' she added with a frown. 'It makes me uncomfortable to think of someone watching my every move.'

Gregorio would rather Lia felt a little discomfort than any harm came to her. If Richardson thought for one moment she knew of his duplicity there was no knowing what he would do. For the moment the other man felt secure, with his funds in an offshore company, but if Richardson ever began to doubt that security that might quickly change.

'Gregorio?'

He grimaced. 'Your father would have wanted someone to take care of you.'

She raised auburn brows. 'I doubt he ever imagined it would be you.'

'No,' he conceded wryly. 'Am I allowed a goodnight kiss?'

Lia burst out laughing. Which was pretty incredible after the conversation she'd just had with this man. But she couldn't help her response. It was so ludicrous for a man like Gregorio to *ask* if he could do something he had decided he wanted to do.

'When did you last ask a lady's permission to kiss her?'

'Never,' he acknowledged dryly.

She continued to chuckle. 'That's honest, anyway.'

'Your answer…?'

Despite the lightness of Gregorio's tone, Lia could sense his inner tension. It was there in his expression, in the stiff set of his shoulders and the hands clenched at his sides.

Long and elegant hands she had found herself studying as they ate dinner together. Everything about Gregorio was elegant and controlled. The way he moved. The way he ate. The way he talked. All calmly and elegantly done, and all firmly under his control.

A part of Lia wanted to shake that control—if only for a few minutes.

Besides, it was very narrow in this hallway, and made even more so by Gregorio's physically overwhelming presence. She could feel the heat of his body so close to her own, and breathe in that seductive aftershave…

'Yes.' She looked directly into his fathomless black eyes.

His brows rose. 'Yes?'

Lia felt a smile parting her lips. It felt good to smile again. In a genuine show of happiness rather than the polite curving of her lips she had been showing everyone for months now. Besides, she had just succeeded in surprising the hell out of Gregorio.

'Yes,' she repeated, more firmly.

She didn't need the warmth of another human being tonight, she *wanted* it—and not just anyone's warmth either. Gregorio's. She very badly wanted to know how it felt to be held and kissed by Gregorio de la Cruz.

Gregorio hesitated no longer and moved in closer to Lia, his hands moving up to cup her cheeks as he lifted her face, his gaze holding hers as he slowly lowered and tilted his head to claim her lips with his own.

Soft lips parted slightly beneath his as he continued to kiss her. Tasting. Sipping. Lia's hands moved up to grasp hold of his wrists and she moved up on tiptoe to increase the pressure of her lips against his.

Gregorio felt as if he had been in a constant state of arousal for days...weeks—which he had—and now he was actually kissing Lia again he never wanted to stop.

His arms moved about her waist and he pulled her body in tight against the hardness of his as he deepened the kiss. His tongue swept lightly across and then between her lips to enter the welcoming heat beyond.

It felt as if he was *inside* Lia as she sucked his tongue in deeper still, her cheeks hollowing around his invading tongue in a parody of how it would feel to have him thrusting between her thighs. Hot and wet, and oh-so-good.

Gregorio gave a groan and began to stroke his tongue in and out of her mouth, his arousal throbbing hot and heavy in response as he placed his hands on Lia's bottom and pulled her body in even tighter against his own.

Lia gave a low moan, her breathing ragged as she felt the length of Gregorio's arousal pressing against the softness of her abdomen. Heat built between her thighs in response. Her nipples felt hard as unripe berries, and achingly sensitive against the restricting lace of her bra.

She pressed in closer still as she released Gregorio's wrists to slide her hands up his chest, until her fingers became entangled in the dark and silky hair at his nape. She couldn't seem to get close enough—she wanted more, *ached* for so much more.

Gregorio broke the kiss to trail his lips hotly down the arched column of her throat. 'Can I stay?' he asked throatily. 'Please, Lia, let me—'

'Yes.'

She didn't even allow him to finish. She didn't want to talk—she wanted...*wanted*...him. She wanted Gregorio, and the mindless pleasure she already knew they would have together.

David had been her only lover to date, and Lia had always assumed that her lack of orgasm was a fault on her part, not his. Had thought that they needed time to adjust and become accustomed to each other in that way. That pleasure would come with the physical familiarity of being married to each other.

But just a few minutes of being in Gregorio's arms, of having his lips and hands on her, and Lia felt as if she was about to spontaneously combust. As if something inside her was about to burst free, taking her to a place she had never been before.

'I said yes.' She frowned as Gregorio continued to look at her searchingly.

'Are you going to hate me again in the morning?'

'I might hate you again later on tonight, but right now *hate* is the last thing I'm feeling. Can we not dissect this, Gregorio?' She frowned as those black eyes continued to question her. 'Conversation is very overrated, you know.'

His tension broke as he smiled. 'You *are* going to be bossy in bed,' he decided with satisfaction.

'I'm going to be bossy *out* of bed if we don't go to my bedroom very soon!'

Gregorio chuckled softly as he placed his hands beneath her bottom and lifted her up off the floor. 'Wrap your legs around my waist,' he encouraged.

'Now who's being bossy...?'

Lia trailed off, her breathing becoming erratic as Gregorio turned to walk down the hallway towards her bedroom.

'Oh, God...'

Her arms clung tightly about his neck and she buried her face against his throat as each step he took ground her body sensually against his, sending wave after wave of pleasure coursing through her body.

'That is so... Gregorio!'

She gasped as the tension between her thighs intensified before suddenly being released, engulfing her in heat and an overwhelming pleasure that caused the whole of her body to tremble and shake as she rode out that release to its last shuddering throb.

So *that* was what the ultimate in physical pleasure felt like!

That connection men and women throughout the ages had killed for.

Lia now understood every one of those emotions.

Her orgasm had been a pleasure such as she had never dreamed of. Pure ecstasy. It had connected her to Gregorio in a way she had never experienced before with anyone else.

There was none of the awkwardness or embarrassment she had always felt with David as Gregorio carried her across her darkened bedroom and lay her down on the bed before lying on his side next to her.

'Are you okay?' He lifted a hand to caress the hair back from her temple.

'Better than okay.' She nodded, still trying to catch her breath.

'Light on or off?' he queried softly.

'On,' Lia decided, and she turned to switch on the lamp on her bedside table.

She moved up onto her knees, wanting to see all of Gregorio as she slowly undressed him. That hard and muscled chest. The taut abdomen. The long length of his arousal. Those long and muscular legs.

She already knew he was going to look like

a mythological god. All golden flesh and hard muscles.

'Arms up,' she instructed as she lifted and then removed his T-shirt completely, revealing his chest covered in a light dusting of dark hair, his nipples like bronzed pennies. She touched them lightly, glancing up at him as she heard his sharp intake of breath and felt his nipples pebble against her fingertips. 'You like that?'

'Yes.'

Gregorio had no idea what Lia's sexual experience had been before tonight, and he didn't want to know either. Here and now, the two of them together, it was so highly charged, so intensely pleasurable, that everything and every other woman he had ever known before Lia faded into insignificance. Forgotten. All he could see and feel was narrowed down to this woman. To seeing and feeling only Lia.

Her orgasm a few minutes ago had come as a complete surprise to him. He had barely touched her before she'd found her release.

He could only hope that quicksilver response was uniquely for him.

He sucked in a breath as Lia scraped her nails lightly over the hardness of his nipples, a slight smile curving her lips as she watched and obviously enjoyed seeing his response to her touch.

She could pleasure and torment him for hours if it meant he could see that smile on her lips while she did it.

Her eyes glowed dark grey, her cheeks were flushed, and her lips were curved into that seductive smile, slightly swollen from their earlier kisses.

'Dios!' Gregorio's back arched off the bed as Lia's tongue rasped moistly across one sensitised nipple, his fingers becoming entangled in the auburn hair draped across his chest as her lips completely engulfed his nipple with the heat of her mouth and she suckled deeply.

Gregorio was used to being the lover, the aggressor, and while women always responded with kisses and caresses he had never had one take charge of him in quite this way before. It felt strange, and yet somehow liberating at the same time—a measure of the trust that was slowly building between the two of them. Fragile as yet, but growing stronger the more time they spent together.

The things Lia was doing to him with her mouth and tongue made Gregorio's body throb and ache.

Lia lifted her head to smile at him, her eyes sultry as her hands moved down to unfasten the top button of his jeans, quickly followed by the other three. Gregorio sighed his relief as his desire was no longer constricted by material, only to suck his breath in again as Lia's hand caressed the length of him outlined against his black boxers.

'I want to feel your lips and your hands on my bared flesh,' he encouraged huskily. 'Please...' He lifted himself up and pushed his jeans and boxers down to his thighs.

Lia's breath caught in her throat as her gaze feasted on his fully naked body. She moistened her lips with the tip of her tongue.

'You're— *No...!*' she cried as the ringing of

the doorbell sounded, shrill and intrusive. 'God, no...' she groaned as she buried her face against Gregorio's chest.

'Ignore it—' A second loud ring, longer this time, cut across Gregorio's protest.

'It's probably one of the neighbours, come to say hello to the new tenant.' She sighed as she sat up.

'That has never been my experience.' He frowned.

'That's probably because you live in a hotel. I have to answer that,' Lia snapped with impatience as the bell rang for a third time. Whoever was on the other side of that door was *not* going to receive a warm welcome from her—that was for certain. 'Stay exactly where and how you are,' she instructed Gregorio as she got up from the bed.

'Sí, señorita.' Dark eyes glittered with humour.

Lia cast one last, longing look at the lean and muscular length of Gregorio's body before turning to hurry from the bedroom, straightening her clothes as she went.

The doorbell rang for a fourth time just as she wrenched the door open.

'Oh, thank goodness!' A relieved Cathy stood outside in the hallway, Rick at her side. 'I was *so* worried about you.' She gave Lia a hug.

'I'm fine,' Lia assured her, her mind racing as she wondered what she was going to do about Cathy and Rick standing on her doorstep when Gregorio was half naked in her bedroom.

No immediate answer came to mind.

'You seemed so down at lunch,' Cathy said. 'I was worried about you, and Rick and I just had to come over and see if you were okay.'

'I'm really fine,' Lia repeated distractedly, her mind racing as she tried to find a solution to this dilemma.

There was no way she could get out of inviting Cathy and Rick inside her apartment. Not when they were giving up their evening to visit her. But, conversely, she couldn't expect Gregorio to spend all evening hiding out in her bedroom.

As if that was really an option! Gregorio went where he wanted and did what he wanted. It went without saying that hiding in a woman's bedroom would *not* be what he wanted.

'You look a little flushed.' Cathy looked at her in concern. 'Maybe you have the start of a cold?'

'Er… Cat…' Rick said hesitantly beside her.

'Or maybe it's the flu?' His wife continued to fuss. 'There's a lot of it about at the moment, and—'

'Cat!'

'What is it, Rick?' Cathy turned to her husband impatiently.

Lia winced as Rick ignored his wife and continued to look past Lia into the hallway beyond. She knew without looking that Gregorio had left her bedroom, after all, and was now standing behind her.

She just hoped he had put his clothes back on first!

CHAPTER SIX

'PERHAPS I SHOULD introduce myself?'

A fully dressed Gregorio—thank goodness—looked at Lia as the four of them stood awkwardly in the sitting room of her apartment. Lia really hadn't had any choice but to invite the other couple inside.

'Fine.' It was the only word she'd seemed able to say since she had opened her apartment door and found Cathy and Rick standing outside in the hallway.

'Oh, I know *exactly* who you are, Mr de la Cruz,' Cathy assured him with a sideways glance at Lia. 'We're Cathy and Rick Morton. Friends of Lia's.'

Lia winced as she sensed Cathy's censorious gaze on her after that last announcement. It was questioning why, when they were such close friends, Lia hadn't confided in Cathy regarding her friendship with Gregorio. She was going to have some serious explaining to do once Gregorio had left. Whenever that was going to be. Because of the four of them he seemed to be the most relaxed and the least intimidated by this situation. He also showed no inclination to leave.

Lia felt bad for not telling Cathy about Gregorio's previous visit, or that she was working for him. At the time she had thought it was the right thing to do—that she would be avoiding Gregorio as much as possible in future, so telling Cathy about him was a waste of time. Look how well *that* had turned out!

But at least he had all his clothes back on and had tidied himself before he'd come out of her bedroom. Although the slightly creased T-shirt and tousled dark hair indicated that hadn't been the case minutes ago.

Lia knew Cathy was going to want to kill her once the two of them could speak privately.

'I remember seeing you with Lia at the funeral,' he answered Cathy as the three of them shook hands. 'And, please, you must both call me Gregorio.'

The pleasantries over, an awkward silence once again fell over the room.

'Wine.' Lia had finally found another word to say. 'Let's all have a glass of wine. I have red or white. Which would you prefer? The white is dry, the red fruity.'

Now she'd regained her voice Lia didn't seem able to stop babbling, but at the same time her gaze couldn't quite meet Cathy's or Rick's, and she was avoiding Gregorio's completely.

She felt so stupid. Like a child who had been caught out not being honest. Not that Cathy or Rick were in the least judgemental—it was Lia who felt as if she had somehow disappointed them.

'You sit and chat with your friends and I'll pour the wine.' Gregorio spoke dryly, obviously knowing the topic of their conversation would be him.

'I'll help you.' Rick hurriedly followed the other man into the kitchen area.

'Cathy—'

'He seems to know his way around your kitchen,' Cathy observed softly as the two women sat down, Her brows rose as she watched Gregorio remove a bottle of red wine from the rack before taking glasses from the cupboard above.

Lia tried again. 'Cathy—'

'I have to say he's an improvement on the last guy,' her friend murmured appreciatively.

Lia's eyes widened. It was the last thing she had expected the other woman to say. 'You didn't like David?'

'He was your choice, so of course I liked him.' Her friend shrugged. 'Except I didn't, if you know what I mean.'

No, Lia *didn't* know what she meant. She had always thought Cathy and Rick *liked* David: the four of them had often gone out to dinner together, and they had always seemed to get on.

'He could be rather condescending,' Cathy added with a grimace.

Thinking back to those evenings, she realised David *had* talked down to Cathy and Rick. As if they weren't quite of his social standing. Which was ridiculous. Cathy's father was a politician, currently in government, and Rick's family owned and ran a huge farm in Worcestershire. Rick himself was senior manager at a software firm here in London.

It made her wonder what else she hadn't noticed about David during the months they had dated and been engaged. Whether Gregorio's suspicions about him were well-founded. David had certainly proved himself to be a less than supportive fiancé after her father's death.

Unlike Gregorio…

She might not particularly *like* the idea of Gregorio having his security men keeping an eye on her, but there was also a certain…reassurance—a warmth in knowing that someone cared enough about her to do that.

Lia chewed on her bottom lip. 'About Gregorio—'

'Don't worry about it, sweetie.' Cathy smiled as she leaned forward to give Lia's arm a reassuring squeeze. 'It's a surprise, but not an unpleasant one. The man is *gorgeous*, isn't he?' She lowered her voice even more.

Lia glanced across to where Gregorio and Rick were chatting together like old friends—as it turned out, as she listened briefly to their conversation, they were two men who both liked football but supported opposing teams. Gregorio was laughing at something Rick had said, his dark eyes warm with humour, a relaxed expression lightening his austere features.

'Yes, he is,' Lia acknowledged softly.

'He doesn't seem at all cold and remote this evening,' Cathy added approvingly.

Gregorio had been anything *but* cold and remote in her bedroom a few minutes ago. Burning hot and very close better described the two of them together. Just thinking about all Gregorio's naked and responsive flesh was enough to cause Lia's cheeks to warm in a blush.

Cathy gave her a knowing grin. 'Do you want us to leave as soon as we've drunk our wine?'

'*No!* I mean… No,' she repeated softly as the two men turned curiously at her vehemence. 'I think I may need saving from myself,' she told Cathy with a groan. 'I don't know what I was even thinking. He's just so—'

'Overwhelming and sexy as hell?' her friend supplied lightly.

Lia's gaze could no longer meet Cathy's. 'Yes.'

'Here we go,' Rick announced in an over-hearty voice as he handed Cathy a glass of red wine. No doubt as a warning to the two women that they were no longer alone.

'Lia.'

She glanced up at Gregorio as he stood beside her chair, holding out a glass a red wine for her to take. The humour gleaming in those dark eyes told her he had overheard Cathy's last comment—and Lia's response to it.

She turned her gaze away, her hand shaking slightly as she took the wine glass from him.

'So, what do the two of you have planned for the rest of the evening?' Rick prompted politely—and immediately had to thump Cathy on the back as she began to choke on a mouthful of wine. 'What did I say?' Rick looked bewildered by his wife's reaction.

'Never mind, love,' Cathy answered once she'd caught her breath. 'Let's just drink our wine and pick up a Chinese takeaway on the way home.'

'Lia and I have already eaten, but we could always order in food for you to eat here?' Gregorio suggested lightly. 'Alternatively, we could all go out for a drink together somewhere the two of you could have some food?'

Lia slowly turned her head to look at him. Who *was* this man and what had he done with the cold and arrogant Gregorio de la Cruz? Because *this* man certainly wasn't the ruthless businessman who swallowed up companies with the voracity of a shark. Or the playboy billionaire she'd read about in the newspapers who had a different blonde on his arm every week.

'Okay, this is getting a little weird now.'

Lia stood up decisively. She might have been in shock since Cathy and Rick had arrived, but she was recovering fast. And the four of them spending the rest of the evening together wasn't going to happen.

'Cathy and Rick are far too polite to say so, but they don't want to spend the evening with the two of us—'

'Hey, don't put words in my mouth,' Cathy protested.

'Because they are both totally freaked out right now,' Lia continued determinedly. '*I'm* freaked out right now, so I know they have to be too.' She frowned at Gregorio. 'The two of us aren't a couple and we aren't going out for the evening with anyone—least of all my two best friends. What happened earlier...' She gave Cathy and Rick a self-conscious glance. 'Shouldn't have happened.'

'I believe *you* are the one embarrassing your friends.' Now Gregorio looked every inch the coldly arrogant man Lia had met at her father's funeral: his eyes were narrowed and no longer warm, but hard as the onyx they resembled, and his sculptured lips were thin and unsmiling.

'Not at all.' Cathy stood up. 'It's time the two of us were going anyway. Rick?' she prompted sharply as her husband made no move to get up out of his chair.

'What? Oh. Yes. Sorry.' He rose abruptly to his feet, then seemed to realise he still had a glass in his hand and looked around for somewhere to put it.

'Here.' Cathy took the glass and placed it on the coffee table next to her own. 'I'll call you in the morning, okay?' She gave Lia a hug. 'Nice to meet you, Gregorio.' She nodded. 'Say goodnight, Rick,' she instructed dryly. Her husband still looked slightly dazed by the speed of their departure.

'Goodnight, Rick,' he repeated as he was pulled down the hallway by his wife.

The apartment door closed quietly behind them seconds later.

Leaving an awkward silence.

A very cold and very uncomfortable silence that caused Lia to give a shiver as the chill seemed to seep into her bones.

'Your rudeness was completely uncalled for,' Gregorio snapped finally.

'No.' Lia's chin rose as she faced him. 'No, it really wasn't. I don't know what happened between the two of us earlier, but it isn't going to happen again. I won't *let* it happen again,' she added firmly. She was totally unsettled by their earlier passion. 'And we certainly aren't ever going out for the evening with any of my friends, as if the two of us are together.'

Gregorio was having to exert great willpower so as not to lose his temper. He made a point of never losing his temper—no matter what the provocation. But he had not encountered anyone as stubborn as Lia before.

He had been disappointed when he'd realised Lia's visitors had to be Cathy and Rick Morton, the couple he had seen her with at her father's graveside two months ago. He knew, from the daily security reports he received, that Lia had lived with the other couple before moving into her apartment at the weekend.

Rather than remaining in Lia's bedroom like a dirty little secret she was keeping hidden away, Gregorio had decided to dress and join them.

He had no experience of being in the company of a woman's friends or family, but he had thought he was doing quite well. Being charming to Cathy. Talking football with her husband. Pouring them all wine. It had seemed perfectly logical to him, as the other couple were obviously close to Lia, to suggest they all spend the rest of the evening together.

Lia's vehemently negative response to that suggestion had been immediate. And, to his surprise, her words had hurt.

He was close to his two brothers. Well…as close as he could be when he was based in London, Sebastien was in New York, and Alejandro was taking care of the estate and vineyards in Spain. He also had a large extended family, of which *he* was the recognised patriarch.

He had sex with the women who flitted in and out of his life, but he did *not* become involved with their family or their friends. He rarely even *met* any of their friends, let alone their family. He had been willing to make an exception with

Lia, and he'd received a verbal and public slap in the face for his trouble.

He would not make the same mistake again.

'What happened earlier is that you used me for sex,' he bit out coldly, his accent more clipped in his anger. 'No doubt any man would have sufficed. I am pleased I was able to give you *one* orgasm, at least, before we were interrupted.'

The colour had drained from her cheeks. 'You *bastard*!'

Gregorio shrugged his shoulders. 'You were the one at such pains to explain exactly what we have between us, I am merely agreeing with you. When you feel in the need for sex again perhaps you should give me a call? If I have the time I— No, I do not *think* so.' Gregorio grasped hold of Lia's wrist as her hand arced up towards his cheek. He used that grip to pull her up close against him. 'I warned you the last time you did that I would not allow you to do it again without retaliating.'

Her top lip turned back in a sneer. 'I should

have known you were the type of man who would hit a woman!'

Gregorio's jaw tightened. 'Any man who strikes a woman, for whatever reason, no longer has the right to call himself a man. My retribution will be of quite a different kind, I assure you.'

Lia swallowed. Gregorio's threat was all the more disturbing because he'd delivered it in such a calm and conversational tone. As if they were discussing the weather rather than his retribution.

'Let go of me,' she said evenly.

He quirked one dark brow. 'Are you going to slap me again?'

'No.' That impulse had passed. Besides, she had never felt tempted to hit anyone before Gregorio.

'Pity.' He bared his teeth in a humourless smile as he released her wrist and stepped back. 'I believe I would have enjoyed punishing you. Perhaps I still will...' he mused.

Lia breathed shallowly. 'Punishing me?'

Black eyes glittered through narrowed lids.

'You are not someone who likes to feel out of control, are you?'

That sounded more like a statement than a question, and Lia treated it as such. 'Neither are you,' she defended.

'I do not remember objecting when you made love to me earlier.'

The warmth in her cheeks deepened as she recalled her aggression. And her pleasure...

Which was another reason she wasn't going to allow herself to be alone with Gregorio again. He affected her, drove her wild with passion in a way no other man ever had. Including the man she had intended to marry.

She and David had spent the night together regularly after their engagement. Nights she had enjoyed even as she had known there had to be *more*. Although she had enjoyed David's lovemaking she had never reached the pinnacle of physical pleasure when they were together.

A few minutes of just being kissed by and kissing Gregorio and she'd had her first orgasm. He hadn't even touched her. The stimulation had come from those kisses alone.

Just being with him physically excited her.

As much as it disturbed her.

Because she wasn't sure she even *liked* Gregorio.

Lia moistened her lips with the tip of her tongue. 'I really think you should leave now.'

Gregorio had given her far too much to think about. Not just what had happened between the two of them, but the truth about David's involvement in the demise of her father's company.

Because, no matter how confused she was about her feelings for Gregorio, she knew he wasn't a liar. In fact, he was the opposite: Gregorio tended to be brutally honest.

Lia knew she had to see and talk to David again. To find out for herself if what Gregorio had said about him having a gambling habit was true, at least. To try and get David to tell her the part he had played—or not played—in the downfall of Fairbanks Industries.

CHAPTER SEVEN

'THIS ISN'T PART of my job description.'

Gregorio quirked one dark eyebrow as he looked at Lia, standing in the doorway to the office in his penthouse suite. 'My PA has called in sick this morning. I'm not sure it's altogether wise for you to refuse to assist your employer on only your second day of employment.'

Lia wasn't sure it was either. But neither did she think it was coincidence that Gregorio had requested *she* be the one to assist him. Although he certainly *looked* businesslike, in one of those perfectly tailored suits—dark grey today—with a pale grey shirt and striped blue tie.

After a very disturbed night's sleep Lia had tried to put yesterday evening from her mind and treat today as a new start. It had proved not altogether possible when—as promised—Cathy had telephoned her first thing this morning, wanting to know all the juicy details of Lia's relationship with Gregorio.

Lia had told her friend what she felt comfortable with Cathy knowing. Mainly that she really had no idea what last night had been about. Only that she wasn't going to allow Gregorio that close to her again.

After making another phone call Lia had forced herself to shower and dress before coming in to work today. Knowing that Gregorio might appear at any moment and shake what little self-confidence she had managed to dredge up and wrap around herself like a protective cloak.

Having Michael Harrington send her up to the penthouse floor to assist Mr de la Cruz within minutes of her arrival at the Exemplar Hotel had succeeded in tearing a great hole in that protective cloak!

'Is this what you meant when you spoke about punishing me?'

Gregorio narrowed his eyes as he sat back in his chair to look across the width of his desk at

Lia. She was once again wearing a black business suit and a cream blouse—the uniform of all the hotel receptionists—and her hair was swept up in that confining style he didn't like. Mainly because it hid all the gold and cinnamon highlights amongst the red. Her face was slightly pale, but there was a defiant glitter in those dark grey eyes.

'You consider assisting your employer to be a punishment?' he challenged.

'That would depend on what he wants my assistance with.'

'The history and accounts of some of the companies I am interested in buying.'

Her eyes widened. 'And why would you think I have any knowledge on either of those subjects?'

Gregorio gave a confident smile. 'Because your father told me you very often assisted him when he worked at home in the evenings.'

Her hand reached out blindly to allow her fingers to grasp hold of the doorframe for support. 'My father told you…?'

'Jacob and I met several times.' He nodded. 'Once we had finished our business discussions you invariably came into the conversation.' He stood up to move around to the front of his desk. 'He was very proud of you.'

Lia could find no answer to that statement. Instead she blinked back the tears stinging her eyes and prompted briskly, 'Just tell me what I can do to help you.'

Gregorio had to bite back his immediate response. Which was, *you can get down on your knees and relieve me of the throbbing ache of arousal that kept me awake all night.* He was pretty sure that wasn't the sort of help Lia was offering.

He had been coldly angry when he'd left Lia's apartment the evening before. Something that seemed to have become a common occurrence around Lia. A couple of glasses of brandy had eased some of that anger, but nothing had succeeded in taking away the sexual tension that had kept his body hard and throbbing for release.

Not even a freezing cold shower.

The moment he thought of Lia again—and that was becoming an occupational hazard too—his desire sprang back to life as if it had never gone away.

Receiving a phone call earlier this morning from Tim, his PA, explaining that he was sick with the flu, had seemed to set the tone for today too.

Until Gregorio had realised exactly *which* member of the hotel staff he could ask to assist him in Tim's place...

Was it a punishment for Lia for the fact that he couldn't seem to stop wanting her?

Maybe. Whatever his motive, Gregorio already knew that the next few hours were going to be as painful for him as they would for Lia. If for different reasons.

He had been aware of Lia's perfume the moment she entered the penthouse: that light floral scent with an underlying note of womanly musk. And he couldn't stop his gaze from returning again and again to the swell of her breasts, visible where the top two buttons of her blouse had been left unfastened.

They had been interrupted yesterday evening

before he'd had a chance to remove any of Lia's clothing. He had not been allowed to see those breasts bared. His jaw clenched and his teeth ached with how much he wanted to remove her blouse and bra before gorging himself on her naked breasts. Starting with her plump and soon-to-be-aroused nipples…

'The files are on Tim's desk,' he said stiffly instead.

If he had set out to punish Lia, as she'd suggested, then during the course of the morning, working so closely with her, Gregorio knew that his intention had come back to bite him on the butt. Or on another part of his anatomy that was even more sensitive.

Despite the fact that she was sitting across the room from him, at Tim's desk, her perfume continued to fill the air and invade his senses. And Gregorio was aware of every move she made— especially when she stretched her back and arched her neck to ease the tension of sitting at a desk for several hours.

Physical awareness danced along his skin every

time she spoke to him, even on such a mundane subject as company accounts.

Flu or not, Tim had better be back tomorrow, or he could start looking for another job!

'I'm scheduled to have an early lunch today.'

'What?' Gregorio scowled across the room at her.

'Michael has given me an early lunch today,' Lia repeated as she glanced at her wristwatch. 'I'm meeting someone just after twelve.'

'Who?' The demand was out before Gregorio's brain had connected with his mouth. 'We still have work to do,' he added with a scowl.

'I'm entitled to a lunchbreak,' she reasoned. 'I'll make sure I finish here when I get back.' She stood up to push her chair neatly beneath the desktop, making no attempt to answer his query as to who she was meeting for lunch.

Gregorio scowled his frustration. He wanted to tell Lia that she couldn't go. That it was more important that they finish this work and he would order lunch for them both to be brought up by room service.

Most of all I want to know who she's having lunch with!

'Say hello to Cathy for me,' he tested lightly.

Lia's smile was enigmatic. 'I'm not meeting Cathy for lunch, but I'll be sure to pass your message along the next time I speak to her.'

Gregorio stood, feeling too restless to remain seated at his desk. 'Are you going anywhere nice?'

She shrugged. 'Just a little Italian bistro quite close to here.'

Gregorio thought he knew the place she meant. It was tucked away in a side street a couple of blocks from here, and run by a middle-aged Italian couple. The food was both good and inexpensive. Something Lia no doubt now took into consideration with her changed circumstances.

'I could order some chocolate cake from Mancini's to be delivered here,' he tempted.

Her smile was rueful as she shook her head. 'I'm happy with the selection of cheesecakes at the bistro.'

Gregorio's eyes narrowed. 'Do you go there often?'

'I used to in the past, yes,' she answered cautiously.

'With David Richardson?' The offices of Richardson, Richardson and Pope weren't too far from here, so it seemed logical to assume that Lia might have met her fiancé for lunch at the bistro for the sake of convenience.

Lia frowned. 'You may be my employer, but I don't believe that where I have lunch and who with, in my own time, is any of your business.'

Of course it wasn't. And Gregorio was well aware that his questions were intrusive. It wouldn't even have occurred to him to ask another employee about their lunch plans. Tim had worked for him for two years now, and the two men worked well together, but he had zero interest in Tim's private life.

But Lia wasn't only his employee.

She was also the woman Gregorio wanted, and he wanted her more the more time he spent in her company.

Which meant it was time—*past* time—to call one of the women he'd occasionally had lunch with in the past. An afternoon in bed with another woman would certainly ease his physical frustration.

Having made that decision, Gregorio found himself still in his office fifteen minutes later, waiting for the call from one of his security team to tell him exactly who Lia was meeting for lunch.

Lia hadn't known how she would feel when she saw David again—the first time they had met since the evening he'd broken their engagement. David had been in Scotland—conveniently?—when she'd buried her father, and his own father had represented Richardson, Richardson and Pope. It had been an awkward situation for both of them, and they hadn't spoken apart from Alec Richardson's murmured condolences as he moved along with the procession of other people offering their sympathies for her loss.

Her first thought, when David entered the bistro where they had agreed to meet for lunch, was that he looked different from how she remembered him.

Or maybe she was just looking at him from another perspective? Through lenses that were less rose-coloured? After all, she had once thought herself in love with this man.

What a difference three months could make. What a difference *one evening* had made: David had shattered every one of her illusions about him when he'd walked out of her life and left her to the mercy of the media wolves.

He was still male-model-handsome. His hair was the colour of ripened corn, his eyes as blue as the sky on a summer's day. His body looked lithe and fit in his tailored dark suit, and he wore a blue shirt that was perfectly matched in colour for his eyes, and a meticulously knotted navy blue tie.

Yes, on the surface David still gave the appearance of being a confidently handsome lawyer. But Lia was able to look past that veneer today. To see the lines of dissipation beside his eyes and mouth. The slight laxness to the skin about his jaw. To note that his strides through the bistro seemed less purposeful and more full of nervous energy.

Was that an indication that David was far from comfortable with this meeting that Lia had requested when she'd rung him earlier that morning?

It was a meeting he had tried to avoid, and only acquiesced to once Lia had explained that she had found some papers amongst her father's things she thought David might be interested in seeing. It wasn't true, of course, but the fact that he had changed his mind about the meeting based on that comment had filled Lia with misgivings. Perhaps the things Gregorio had told her about David were the truth, after all.

David was a thief and a liar...

'You're looking well,' David commented, but he made no move to touch her or to kiss her in greeting before sliding into the seat opposite hers in this relatively private booth at the back of the bistro.

Lia didn't return the compliment. Mainly because it wasn't true. 'I'm very well, thank you,' she answered with cool formality.

He waited until they had placed their drinks order with the waitress and she had left them menus before asking, 'Are you still living with the Mortons?'

'I have an apartment of my own in town now. And a job,' Lia added.

'One that pays actual wages or another job at one of your do-good charities?'

Cathy was right, Lia realised. David *did* condescend. He was doing it right now.

Her fingers itched to wipe the mocking smile off his lips.

When had she developed these violent tendencies?

She had never struck anyone in her life until she'd lashed out at Gregorio in that restaurant. Now she wanted nothing more than to slap David too.

Was it because she knew, deep down, that Cathy's comments about him had been correct?

That Gregorio's suspicions about David's involvement in her father's downfall might also prove to be correct...?

'I'm a hotel receptionist.'

The words instantly made her think of the morning she had just spent, working in Gregorio's penthouse suite.

The suite was furnished differently from the others Lia had been shown around on her first morning—it was part of her job as a receptionist to know exactly what each of the rooms had to offer people wanting to stay at the hotel. And the office was definitely personal to Gregorio, indicating that he really did live there all the time.

It made a certain sense. Gregorio had all the conveniences of the hotel—like room and laundry service, restaurants, a spa, et cetera—and none of the inconvenience that came along with owning his own house or apartment.

Even if it *had* seemed a little strange to know that his bedroom was just down the hallway from where the two of them were working...

'How the mighty have fallen,' David sneered.

The gloves really *had* come off today, hadn't they?

It made Lia feel slightly foolish for not having seen David's true nature before now. No doubt he had hidden the worst parts of himself from her while they were dating and then engaged, but even so Lia had always believed herself a good judge of character. Obviously she had been wrong.

Had she been wrong about Gregorio being the bad guy?

She'd already acknowledged that might be the case.

Now she was convinced of it.

Quite what she was going to do about it, she had no idea. Gregorio was…overwhelming. Forceful. And he made no secret of his desire for her.

At least he *hadn't*…

But the way they had parted last night, and the stiltedness between them this morning, seemed to indicate he might have put that feeling behind him and moved on.

Could she blame him?

He had been very polite and friendly with Cathy and Rick last night—*she* was the one who had been rude and dismissive towards *him*. In front of the other couple. No wonder Gregorio had been so angry.

She owed him an apology, Lia realised.

'Lia…?'

She narrowed her gaze on the man sitting opposite her. 'Did you ever love me or were you just using me from the start?'

David looked taken aback by her direct attack. 'The niceties are over, I take it?'

'Very much so.' She nodded abruptly. 'So answer the question. Were you using me, and my father's name and wealth, right from the start of our relationship?'

His scowled. 'I only agreed to meet with you today because you said you had some papers you needed to discuss with me.' His eyes narrowed. 'There *are* no papers, are there?'

'No.'

'Damn it.' He swore softly under his breath.

'I have no intention of hashing over ancient history—'

'It's only been a few months, David,' she snorted. 'I would hardly call that ancient *anything*!'

Their conversation stopped briefly while the waitress put their drinks down on the table. Lia shook her head when the young girl asked if they were ready to eat yet. Lia very much doubted they would get as far as eating anything. Just the thought of food made her feel nauseous.

David leaned forward across the table once the two of them were alone again. 'I don't appreciate being spoken to by you in this insulting manner.'

Her eyes narrowed. 'And *I* don't *appreciate* learning that I was going to marry a dissolute gambler!'

David reared back, a look of total shock on his face. 'I have no idea what you're talking about.'

But he did, Lia realised. The truth was there in his guarded expression and in the way his face had paled.

'Let's not play any more games, David,' she

scorned. 'Your parents can't possibly know about your gambling, or they would have done something to help you.'

She had always liked the couple she had believed would one day be her in-laws, and knew that Daphne and Alec Richardson would be devastated to learn the truth about their only child.

'Are you threatening me?'

Lia felt a shiver down the length of her spine at the underlying malice in David's tone. It reminded her of something her father had once told her: a cornered animal almost always attacked. The look of rage on David's face said he was getting ready to do just that.

'Not at all,' she assured him smoothly. 'I was merely thinking how disappointed they would be if they knew the sort of man you really are.'

'Stay away from my parents!' David grated.

'I intend to. Oh, I almost forgot.' Lia turned to search through her handbag. 'You might want to give this to the next unsuspecting idiot.' She placed a ring box down on the table in front of him. The engagement ring inside had belonged to his grandmother. 'Or perhaps you could just sell it to pay off more of your gambling debts? But then, you don't need to, do you?' she continued in a hard voice. 'Not when you have the money you stole from my father's company stashed away in an offshore account.'

'You don't... I didn't... You can't possibly know...' David's face was now an ashen grey rather than just white.

'I *do* know. And, yes, you *did* do exactly what I've just accused you of doing. I don't have all the proof as yet, but I will. Believe me, I *will*,' she assured him vehemently.

She would never wish to harm Daphne and Alec deliberately by revealing the truth about their son, but neither could she allow David to get away with having destroyed her father.

'I don't think so,' David sneered as he recovered quickly. 'You're no longer the privileged daughter of the wealthy and powerful Jacob Fairbanks. Now you're just Lia Fairbanks, who has to work for a living. You have all the power and influence of a toothless dog.'

'You—'

'Sorry I'm a little late, Lia.'

Lia had recognised Gregorio's voice the instant he spoke, but that didn't stop her from staring at him as he slid into the seat beside her. Or drawing in a shocked breath as he kissed her lightly on the lips before turning his narrowed gaze on the man seated on the opposite side of the table.

'Richardson.' He nodded tersely.

If Lia was surprised at Gregorio's being there then David had obviously gone into complete shock. So much so he couldn't even answer the other man.

Gregorio turned to Lia, one dark brow raised in innocent query. 'Have you said something to upset your ex-fiancé? What's this?' He picked up the dark blue velvet ring box and flicked the lid open to reveal the two-carat solitaire diamond ring David had given her on their engagement. 'No wonder you gave it back—it isn't right for you at all.' Gregorio snapped the lid closed and put the box back where he had found it. 'I much prefer the natural yellow diamond ring *I* have picked for you.'

The ring Gregorio had picked for *her*?

A natural *yellow* diamond?

Lia had only read about natural yellow diamonds, and seen photographs of them. They were so unique, so rare, that most reputable jewellers claimed they never expected to see one in their lifetime, let alone have the privilege of selling one.

Gregorio reached over and linked his fingers with those of her left hand before lifting it up and kissing her ring finger. 'It's going to look perfect on you.'

'What...? I... You... Are the two of you...?' David at least made an attempt at speech, even if not very successfully.

Talking was still beyond Lia. It was surprise enough that Gregorio had come to the bistro at all, but that he should now be giving David the impression that the two of them were... That they were...

'Yes, we are,' Gregorio stated challengingly.

'Have the two of you ordered yet?' he continued, as if he *hadn't* just rendered the two people
seated at the table with him dumb. 'I worked up
quite an appetite this morning.'

The look he gave Lia could only be called intimate.

Except...

When Lia looked into his eyes she could see
the dangerous glitter so at odds with his pleasant tone and demeanour. Gregorio was angry.
Coldly, furiously angry.

With her? Because she had met up with David?

Lia was pretty sure that was the reason.

Earlier she had refused to tell Gregorio who
she was meeting for lunch, but she'd never had
any intention of keeping the identity of that person a secret: how could she when she knew one
of Gregorio's men would have followed her when
she'd left the hotel earlier? Lia had known that
the other man would report back to Gregorio as
to *who* she was meeting. She just hadn't expected
it to be so soon—or that, knowing she was meeting David, Gregorio would decide to join them.

Or that he would intentionally give David the impression that the two of them were *together*.

What on earth was all that about?

Did Gregorio think David would physically hurt her?

Why else would he have assigned one of his own bodyguards to protect me?

Before today Lia would have dismissed the idea of David ever hurting her as ridiculous. But the dangerous glitter in his eyes a few minutes ago, when he had taken her comment about his parents as a threat, said she would have been wrong.

David was more than capable of hurting her.

And Gregorio was obviously taking no chances.

His protectiveness really was quite… Well, not sweet, because Gregorio was the least *sweet* man Lia knew. But his concern for her definitely gave her a warm and fuzzy feeling inside.

'No, we haven't ordered yet.' She gave him a warm smile. 'I'm not sure David is staying.'

Her ex-fiancé was still staring at Gregorio, and at their linked hands, as if he had seen a ghost. Or his own demise? David must surely realise that with Gregorio beside her—literally—she wasn't the defenceless little nobody he had implied she was earlier.

He gave himself a visible shake before answering her. 'You're right. I have to get back to the office.' He slid to the end of the bench seat.

'Don't forget to take this with you.' Gregorio picked up the ring box, but retained his hold on it as David would have taken it from him. 'Stay away from Lia in future, Richardson.' Gregorio spoke softly, but he was no less threatening because of it. 'If I see you near her again I might not be quite so understanding.'

David's face flushed with annoyance. '*She* was the one who asked for this meeting.'

'Lia always tries to see the good in everyone.' Gregorio nodded. '*I* don't suffer with the same affliction.'

The other man's chin rose defensively at the challenge in Gregorio's tone. 'You don't frighten me.'

'I have no intention of frightening you,' Gregorio said pleasantly as he finally released the ring box. 'But *they* can—and will if I think it neces-sary.' He gave a nod in the direction of the two men standing outside the restaurant.

Lia had to choke back a laugh as she saw the look of horror on David's face as he looked at the two burly bodyguards. One of them had obviously accompanied her, and Gregorio had brought the second man with him. Both men were at least five inches over six feet in height, with shoulders that looked to be almost as broad.

David didn't say another word, pushing the ring box into his jacket pocket as he turned on his heel and strode out of the bistro. Lia saw him give the two bodyguards a wary glance before he hurried off in the direction of his office building.

Leaving a tense silence behind him.

Lia shot Gregorio a nervous glance from be-neath her lashes. She could feel his tension, and see it in the stiff set of his shoulders. His eyes were narrowed, his lips thinned.

She breathed in deeply before speaking. 'I thought—'

'You didn't *think* at all,' Gregorio rasped. 'If

you had then you would have known not to arrange to see or speak to Richardson alone.'

'I—'

'You will *not* defy me in this way again, Lia,' he bit out evenly. 'Do you understand me?'

'But—' She broke off as the unfortunate waitress chose that moment to come back and take their order.

'We are not staying,' Gregorio informed her abruptly as he took out his wallet to remove some money, handing it to the waitress as he slid out of the booth and pulled Lia with him.

'Where are we going?' She just had time to grab her shoulder bag as he marched them both towards the exit.

'Somewhere we can talk privately,' came the grimly determined reply.

Lia didn't like the sound of that.

At all.

CHAPTER EIGHT

'WILL YOU JUST ease up—before I either fall over
or you pull my arm out of its socket?' Lia complained as Gregorio continued his march down
the street, his fingers firmly around the top of
her arm as he pulled her along beside him. Everyone instinctively stepped out of his way, and consequently hers too. They obviously knew from
looking at Gregorio's face not to get in his way.

His expression was… Dark and dangerous.
That was the only way Lia could think of to describe it. Thunderous brows were lowered over
even darker and stormier eyes, his jaw was tight,
lips still thinned, his jaw clenched. His whole
body language said, *Get out of my way or risk
being trampled underfoot.*

An impression no doubt added to by the two

men who were six and half feet of pure muscle following just a couple of steps behind them.

'Gregorio—'

'It would be better if you did not speak to me right now,' he bit out, without so much as glancing at her.

'But—'

'*Dios*, do you *ever* do as you are told?' He maintained his hold on her arm as he turned to face her, his eyes glittering darkly as he glowered at her from his superior height. 'Do you have *any* idea what you risked by meeting Richardson alone?'

She did now. 'I wasn't exactly *alone* when one of your men follows me everywhere I go. Besides, David would never—' She broke off with a wince, knowing that the David she had met today was not the man who had wooed and won her. Today he had been that cornered animal. Feral. Likely to strike out and maim or kill without warning.

Gregorio eyed her scornfully. 'Do not try to

convince me of something you no longer believe yourself!'

Her cheeks warmed. 'That isn't true—'

'Do you still have feelings for him? Is that it?' Gregorio snapped disgustedly. 'You want to believe he is not involved because you are still in love with him?'

'No!'

Gregorio couldn't miss the vehemence in her denial. 'Then why meet with him at all? Why would you even *do* something like that when I have told you of my suspicions regarding him?'

'Because I needed to know—to see for myself—whether or not David is capable of doing what you suspect he has!' She glared at him.

'And?'

She gave a shiver. 'He's more than capable. In fact I was about to excuse myself from having lunch with him when you arrived and started acting like a caveman.'

Given the circumstances, Gregorio considered his behaviour earlier to have been quite circumspect. What he had really wanted to do was rip

David Richardson's head from his shoulders for daring to so much as breathe the same air as Lia.

If Lia thought he had behaved like a caveman when he'd joined her and Richardson, then she should have seen him when he'd first received Silvio's phone call telling him exactly who she was meeting for lunch.

Gregorio had left the hotel immediately and walked the short distance to the bistro. Seeing Lia sitting cosily in a booth with Richardson had only made him angrier. Overhearing Richardson's scornful comments to her, mocking her social fall and her need to work for a living, had made Gregorio want to slam his fist into the other man's face.

'I consider myself to have been very restrained,' he assured her tightly.

'Is your restraint an excuse for all that nonsense about an engagement ring too?' She eyed him disgustedly.

Gregorio felt warmth staining his cheeks. 'It was my way of letting Richardson know that you aren't alone in the world, no matter what he may think to the contrary.'

'By giving him the impression that I'm now engaged to *you*?'

A nerve pulsed in his jaw. 'It worked, didn't it?'

'And what if he decides to tell someone else about our bogus engagement? Maybe the media?' Lia challenged. 'Did you even think of that?'

Of course Gregorio hadn't thought of that. His only objective had been to protect Lia.

Really?

Was he being honest with himself?

Knowing Lia was with David Richardson had filled him with a blinding rage. Seeing her in the company of the other man, her hair a loose tumble about her shoulders in the way that he liked it, had sent every thought from his head except getting rid of Richardson.

And one word.

Mine.

Lia *was* his—whether she knew it yet or not.

Perhaps it was time that she did.

'Gregorio!' Lia squeaked in protest when he

didn't answer her but instead resumed pulling her along the street beside him, his face set in grim lines.

Lia wasn't sure she altogether trusted that expression. And she felt even less reassured when they entered the hotel through the underground car park, where one of the lifts for the penthouse floor was situated. Gregorio scanned his key card to open the doors and pressed the button for the penthouse floor once they were both inside.

Lia could only assume the two bodyguards would either remain downstairs or come up later. Because Gregorio obviously wasn't willing to let them travel in the same lift as them.

Lia could feel the heat and tension radiating from Gregorio now they were together in this small confined space. He didn't so much as look at her—because he was so disgusted with her?—but his harsh expression said he was every inch the arrogant and ruthless Gregorio de la Cruz at this moment.

She ran the tip of her tongue over the dryness of her lips before speaking. 'I believe I owe you an apology for the way I behaved and spoke to you yesterday evening—'

Her words were cut off abruptly as Gregorio pressed her back against one of the mirrored walls, grasping both her wrists in one of his hands before lifting her hands above her head and holding them there as he fiercely claimed her lips with his own.

The length of his body was pressed intimately against Lia's, allowing her to feel how aroused he was. And she was aware of the response of her own body.

She kissed him back with all the pent-up emotions from last night and from this morning, parting her lips to allow Gregorio's tongue to claim the heat of her mouth. Possessively. The victor with his captive. Exactly like that conquistador Lia had once likened him to.

She loved it.

Was she *falling in love* with Gregorio?

It was far too soon for her to know that for sure. Besides, right here and right now she just wanted to kiss and devour him in the same way he was claiming her. To lose herself in the desire that was never far away when the two of them were together.

She pressed even closer against him as she returned heated kiss for heated kiss. Neither of them was even aware of it when the lift doors opened and then closed again—until the lift started to go back down again.

'Dios mio!' Gregorio reluctantly dragged his mouth from Lia's, his forehead resting on hers as he kept her pressed up against the wall. 'You are driving me so crazy we risk being stuck in this lift for the rest of the day.'

Lia laughed softly under her breath. 'I'd much rather we spent our time in a bed!'

Gregorio drew his breath in sharply. 'Me too.'

She smiled teasingly. 'That's it? Just "me too"?'

He grimaced. 'As you said, conversation seems to be our downfall. I do not want to ruin the moment as I obviously did yesterday evening.'

She sobered. 'That was completely my fault. I felt defensive after Cathy and Rick arrived. But I should never have talked to you in that way.' She moistened lips slightly swollen from the force of their kisses. 'You drive me crazy too, Gregorio.'

'I—'

Gregorio turned away as the lift reached the ground floor and the doors opened automatically to reveal a surprised Silvio and Raphael, waiting outside.

Gregorio made no move to separate himself from Lia. 'Could you inform Mr Harrington that Miss Fairbanks will be spending the rest of the day with me in my suite?' he told them, before once again pressing the button for the penthouse floor.

Lia giggled, and buried her face against Gregorio's chest as the lift doors closed and they began their second ascent in as many minutes.

Gregorio had never heard Lia giggle before. It was pleasant. Warming.

An indication that she was happy?

Dios, he hoped so. Because there was no way he was going to be able to let her walk away from him again today.

Lia's confidence faltered slightly as they

stepped out of the lift into Gregorio's suite. He was ten years older, and so much more experienced than she was. He'd had dozens of lovers, whereas she'd only had one—and not a very satisfactory one at that.

She had believed sexual compatibility to be of minor importance when she'd been with David. They'd loved each other, mixed in the same social circles, and their families had approved of the match. Her lack of sexual pleasure with David hadn't seemed that important.

What an idiot I was.

A stupid, naïve idiot who, after reaching a climax in Gregorio's arms while still fully clothed, couldn't wait to experience that sexual release again.

David had always ensured he took his own pleasure, but what if she couldn't satisfy Gregorio? What if—?

'You think too much.' Gregorio reached up and smoothed the frown from her brow. 'First we will take a shower together.'

He clasped her hand in his as they walked down the hallway.

Was Gregorio expecting her to take all her clothes off and get in the shower with him?

Lia had a sick feeling in the pit of her stomach. She had seen photographs of the women Gregorio usually went to bed with, and although she took care of her body she knew she didn't match up to those model-thin, toned-bodied blondes. Despite her weight loss, her breasts were firm and up-tilting, but a little too big for the slenderness of her waist. Her hips were too curvy—

'You are still thinking too much,' Gregorio murmured indulgently, turning to face her as the two of them stood in the middle of the terracotta-tiled bathroom. 'You are very beautiful, Lia.'

He gently claimed her lips with his. Sipping. Tasting. *Claiming.*

Lia was so lost in her rising desire she wasn't even aware of Gregorio removing her jacket, and then unfastening her blouse before dropping it to the floor with her jacket. Or of his unfastening of the zip of her skirt before that too slid down to join her jacket and blouse.

Heat blazed in her cheeks as Gregorio ended their kiss, stepping back, making her painfully aware that she was now wearing only a cream bra and matching panties, along with suspenders and stockings. And for some inexplicable reason she was still wearing her high-heeled shoes!

Lia wondered what Gregorio saw as his hands tightened about hers. His eyes were dark as he looked his fill of her from the top of her head to her ridiculous high-heeled shoes.

'You are every one of my fantasies come to life,' he approved darkly.

Lia somehow doubted that. 'Aren't you a bit overdressed for taking a shower?' she said lightly, changing the subject.

He released her hands and stepped back and out of his shoes before stretching his arms out at his sides. 'Undress me. No—keep your shoes on,' he added gruffly as she would have stepped out of them.

'Now who's bossy?' she teased.

'Those high heels are *very* sexy.'

The burning in her cheeks seemed to have become a permanent fixture as Lia slipped the jacket from Gregorio's shoulders and down his arms before placing it neatly on the vanity: the suit had probably cost more than Lia was going to earn in a month.

His eyes glittered down at her as she stepped forward to unfasten and remove his tie before undoing the buttons on his shirt.

Lia's breath caught in her throat as she bared his chest, her fingers caressing lightly over that olive-toned flesh as she took off his shirt. His body really was beautiful—as perfect as any sculpture of a Greek god and yet, unlike a statue, warm and firm to the touch.

Her fingers were slightly clumsy as she unfastened the button of his trousers and tugged the zip down. The material slid down his hips and thighs before he stepped out of the trousers altogether, revealing that he wore a pair of black boxers beneath, the bulge of his arousal once again visible against the fitted material.

Forget all the gods: Gregorio was pure perfection.

Wide shoulders, toned pecs and abs, long muscular legs...

Just looking at him made Lia's heart beat faster and louder.

'Take them off.'

Lia's breathing became ragged as she raised her hands to the waistband of Gregorio's boxers, hooking a finger at each hip before slowly pulling the material downwards. Which, considering Gregorio's large and obvious erection, wasn't as easy as it sounded.

She had to ease and stretch the material over that pulsing flesh, before falling down on her knees in front of him as she slowly moved the material downwards and then off completely, along with his socks.

Her gaze returned hungrily to Gregorio's fully engorged and fiercely jutting arousal.

'Lia...!'

She knew what Gregorio wanted, what his

husky voice was begging for. Not demanding. *Begging*.

Had Lia fallen to her knees deliberately? For just this purpose?

Absolutely.

She wanted to hear Gregorio's groans of pleasure as she took him into her mouth. To taste and lick him. To suck him.

Just thinking of that, and of how the two of them must look right now—Gregorio completely naked and fully aroused, her wearing only bra, panties and stockings—caused her own level of desire to increase achingly.

Gregorio drew his breath in sharply, his knees almost buckling as he watched Lia's fingers encircle him. She slowly licked her parted lips before bending forward to take him into the heat of her mouth.

His hands moved, his fingers grasping her bared shoulders as her other hand cupped him beneath his arousal. At the same time she took him deeper into the heat of her mouth. She pulled back again—slowly, firmly—her tongue a hot rasp over the sensitive tip, her cheeks hollowed as she sucked.

Gregorio thought the top of his head was going to explode as Lia set a tortuous rhythm. Taking all of him, deeply. Followed by the slow and tormenting drag of withdrawal. The continuous hot stroke of her tongue on his sensitised flesh. The rhythmic squeeze of her hands.

And all the while she looked so damned sexy in her bra, panties and stockings, her hair a wild tumble of auburn, gold and cinnamon about her shoulders, Gregorio couldn't take his eyes off her.

He could feel the heat of his release building, every muscle in his body straining as he fought for control of that release. The pleasure was too much…too much—

'No…!' He pushed her away from him, fingers digging into the soft flesh of her shoulders when she looked up at him with sensual dark eyes. 'Lia…' He pulled her up to her feet, his arms going about her waist as he drew her in tightly against him. 'That was incredible.'

Oral sex had been a definite no-no with David, so this was the first time Lia had ever…

Having no interest in exploring the boundaries of their sexual relationship was surely another sign that David had just been using her.

What an idiot she had been!

'I liked it too,' Lia acknowledged huskily.

'I do not want it to be over too soon.'

Gregorio gave one of those sensual smiles that transformed his face from austere to breathtaking.

'My turn,' he murmured with satisfaction, and he reached behind her and unfastened her bra before removing it completely. *'Dios!'* He spoke almost reverently as his gaze feasted on her pertly bared breasts. 'I love these…' His hands cupped beneath her breasts as he lowered his head to suckle each engorged nipple in turn.

Lia groaned, clinging to Gregorio's shoulders as she was engulfed in pleasure, heat instantly spreading to her core.

'I want to taste you…'

Gregorio straightened before lifting her up in

his arms and carrying her out of the bathroom and down the hallway to his bedroom. He lay her down carefully on the bed, kneeling beside her to hook his thumbs in her panties, pulling them slowly down over her hips and thighs and then off completely, leaving Lia dressed only in the suspenders and stockings.

His eyes darkened as he looked at her. 'You are the sexiest woman—'

'You've seen today?' she teased, sure that Gregorio had been with women a lot sexier than her.

He tilted his head as he studied her. 'Why do you do that? Is it your way of pushing me away?'

She gave a splutter of laughter at the ridiculousness of that statement when they were both naked. 'Do I *look* as if I'm pushing you away?'

Gregorio didn't return her smile. 'We both have pasts, Lia. I can no more take mine away than you can. But there is just the two of us here. Now. Together.' He lay down on the bed beside her, his hand cupping her cheek as he turned her face towards him. 'Beauty is in the eye of the beholder,

Lia, and you are the most beautiful woman it has been my privilege to make love to.'

Her cheeks heated, although at the same time she still felt sceptical. 'I think we're both agreed that it's best if we don't talk.'

'Because you do not believe me?'

'Gregorio—'

'It is okay.' His thumb caressed her full bottom lip. 'I have every intention of showing you how beautiful you are to me.'

And if that was Gregorio's intention then that was exactly what he did as he made love to her tenderly, appreciatively, *savagely.* Squeezing and caressing her breasts as he drove her wild with his lips and tongue, driving Lia over the edge of release time and time again. Until she was so sensitised that his lightest touch inflamed her senses and she crashed into another orgasm.

And still she hungered for more. More of Gregorio's lovemaking. More of *him.*

'I need to be inside you *now,*' he finally rasped, his hair tousled from where Lia had grabbed hold of its darkness at the height of her pleasure.

'Please…' She arched up, needing to be filled, needing to have Gregorio inside her as much as he wanted to be there.

Lia's unease returned during the time it took him to open the foil packet he had taken from the bedside drawer and roll the condom on with an expertise that indicated he had done it many times before.

Gregorio frowned slightly, obviously seeing the uncertainty flickering across Lia's face. 'I realise this is not in the least romantic, but it is my responsibility to protect you.'

There was no arguing with that comment. None that made any sense in the circumstances, anyway.

And Lia totally forgot about that moment of unease as Gregorio knelt between her thighs and slowly, erotically, eased himself into her. Stretching her, filling her, as if they were two parts of a whole, finally joined together.

'That feels so good,' Gregorio groaned as he lay down on top of her, taking his weight on his elbows and claiming her mouth with his as he slowly began to thrust inside her. '*You* feel so good, Lia.'

Lia groaned as Gregorio's movement sent off tiny explosions inside her, wrapping her legs about his waist and pulling him in deeper still. Their breathing became loud and ragged and those thrusts became less co-ordinated as the pleasure built, higher and higher.

Gregorio broke the kiss to groan, his body tense. 'Come with me, *bella*. Now!' he rasped, and he began to pulse inside her, taking Lia with him in an orgasm so strong and intense she screamed out her pleasure.

CHAPTER NINE

'LUNCH HAS ARRIVED.'

Lunch? A glance at her wristwatch told her it was almost five o'clock in the afternoon, and Lia didn't want to move out of the warm comfort of the bed where she and Gregorio had spent the whole afternoon making love. They had left the bed only once, to take the shower they had forgone earlier. Gregorio had made love to her again against the shower wall once they had soaped, washed and caressed each other all over. The third time had been just a few minutes ago.

Every part of Lia ached, but it was a pleasurable ache. An ache that came from knowing Gregorio's possession so intimately, so many times in such a short time.

Which was surprising, because Lia hadn't

thought a man could recover sexually so quickly. David certainly hadn't...

'Whatever you are thinking about has put a frown on your brow,' Gregorio reproved as he crossed the room to stand beside the bed, wearing a towel knotted loosely around his hips.

Probably so that he could open the door when Room Service delivered their late lunch, Lia realised.

'It was nothing of any importance.' And it wasn't. None of it. David. Their less than satisfying relationship. Their broken engagement. *My lucky escape*—that seemed more appropriate. 'I'm too comfortable to get out of bed.' She gave Gregorio a satiated smile.

His smile was indulgent. 'Would you like me to bring the food to you in here?'

'That sounds like an excellent idea.' Lia tucked the sheet about her breasts as she sat up against the pillows.

Gregorio sat on the bed beside her. 'You are very beautiful to me, Lia.' His fingertips ran lightly down one of her flushed cheeks.

Lia believed him this time. How could she not after the exquisite way Gregorio had made love to her for hours? After he had *shown her* time and time again how *beautiful she was to him*.

So why was he now the one frowning?

'I want you to promise me you will not see Richardson alone again.'

Ah.

Gregorio's eyes narrowed. 'Why are you looking at me like that?'

'Probably because I'm wondering if this is the reason you've made love to me all afternoon.' She eyed him suspiciously. 'To distract me, and also so I'd be more amenable to whatever you ask of me.'

He stood up abruptly. 'You have never for a single moment been *amenable*, Lia,' he bit out impatiently. *'Dios mio.'* He ran a hand through his already tousled dark hair. 'Is that what you think of me?' He glared down at her. 'That I would use sex to manipulate you?'

Exactly. *Sex.*

She had been making love...*falling in love...*

while Gregorio had been *having sex*. Very good sex, but nonetheless it was just sex.

Lia wondered why some women—herself included, apparently—had to pretty it up by calling it 'making love'. Maybe because that was exactly what it did—it prettied up what was basically a primal sexual urge. There was a much more crude word Lia could have used to describe it, but she was too much of a lady to use it.

Gregorio scowled his impatience at Lia's lack of a reply. 'I do not remember having to force you into doing anything this afternoon.'

On the contrary, after her initial shyness Lia had proved to be a very adventurous lover. Satisfyingly so.

So why were the two of them arguing again?

Because their conversations *always*—usually sooner rather than later—became an argument. One of them would take umbrage at something the other had said, and a disagreement would ensue.

'I think I should leave.' Lia avoided his gaze, keeping the sheet wrapped about her breasts as she moved to swing her legs out onto the carpeted floor on the other side of the bed.

'Is this how you usually behave?' Gregorio snapped in frustration. 'You run away whenever you are confronted with a situation you cannot control?'

Her eyes flashed as she turned to glare at him. 'I don't have control over a single part of my life right now. Including this part, it seems,' she added vehemently, standing up and taking the sheet with her. 'I no longer *think* I should leave— I *am* leaving.'

She kept the sheet wrapped around her as she marched over to the door.

'Lia!'

She turned in the doorway. 'Let me go, Gregorio.' Tears glistened in her eyes.

Gregorio's shoulders dropped in defeat. He knew he had no desire to force Lia into doing anything. 'As long as you agree not to see Richardson again on your own. My investigation into his lifestyle, and the money missing from your father's company, is still ongoing.'

And Lia's interference would not only put that investigation in jeopardy but also Lia herself.

'You really believe he did it?'

'I do, yes.'

'And that caused my father's heart attack?'

'Yes.'

'Very well.' She nodded. 'But you'll keep me informed?'

'I will,' he conceded tautly. 'Now I insist you allow Silvio to accompany you home and remain outside your apartment building.' After what she had revealed during her conversation with Richardson earlier today, he believed it was now even more necessary that Lia be protected.

She breathed deeply as she obviously fought a battle within herself. 'Do you really think David would hurt me?'

Gregorio's mouth tightened. 'I believe that today you challenged and cornered a man who does not like to be thwarted in any way. By meeting him, saying the things you did, you have now made Richardson aware of some of your suspicions regarding him—if not all of them. It is never a good idea to allow the enemy to know what you are thinking or feeling.'

Lia eyed him quizzically. 'Is that how you've become so successful? By treating everyone else as the enemy?'

He breathed in deeply. 'You are angry with me and deliberately twisting my words.'

Lia was angry with herself—not Gregorio. After all that had happened these past few months she had still allowed herself to be a naïve romantic where Gregorio was concerned. She was twenty-five years old, and had already been used and manipulated by one man for his own selfish purposes. It was time she stopped romanticising and accepted that she and Gregorio had simply spent a pleasurable afternoon in bed together.

And now the afternoon was over.

She forced the tension from her shoulders and half smiled. 'Let's not part as bad friends, hmm, Gregorio?'

Gregorio's eyes narrowed. Friends? Lia believed the two of them to be merely *friends*? After the afternoon they had just spent together?

'Will we be friends with benefits?' he mocked harshly.

'No.' She kept her gaze downcast. 'What happened this afternoon will not happen again.'

'You truly believe that?' he scorned. The sexual tension between them crackled and burned even now. When they were arguing or when they weren't.

She raised her chin as she looked at him, her gaze clear and unwavering. 'It's time I took charge of my own life, Gregorio,' she stated flatly. 'And that includes who I go to bed with.'

'And it will not be me?'

'No.'

Gregorio nodded abruptly. 'Silvio will be waiting downstairs to accompany you when you are ready to leave.'

'Thank you.' Lia disappeared into the hallway, and there followed the sound of the bathroom door closing seconds later.

Gregorio made his call to Silvio and then turned to stare out of the window at the London skyline, his reflection showing him his expression was grim. This afternoon with Lia had been a revelation. She was correct in her belief that in the past twenty years he had bedded many woman. So many he had forgotten some of their names.

He would never forget Lia's name.

Would never forget Lia.

She was unforgettable.

Not because she was the most beautiful woman he had ever seen. Which she was.

Nor because she was the best lover. Which she was.

No, he would never forget her because she was Lia.

Fiery of temperament. Passionate of nature.

Lia.

'What happened to you yesterday—? Careful,' Cathy warned as Lia's hand jerked so suddenly she almost tipped her glass of water all over the table. The two women had met up at the gym after work, and were now enjoying a relaxing cold drink together in the bar there. 'I expected you to telephone last night, but now I really want to know what happened yesterday.'

The other woman eyed Lia knowingly.

'Which part?' Lia couldn't quite meet her friend's gaze.

She had gone to bed early last night—had pulled the covers over her head and slept for almost twelve hours. Today she was back working behind the reception desk at the Exemplar Hotel, so obviously Gregorio's PA had recovered enough to come in today. Or maybe not? Maybe Gregorio was doing the same as Lia? Trying to ignore her existence as she was trying to ignore his. She certainly hadn't seen anything of him in the hotel today.

'The part that's making you blush,' Cathy said with relish.

Lia winced. 'I'd rather not.'

'At least tell me if it involves Gregorio de la Cruz?'

She sighed. 'It does.'

'Wow!' Cathy had a dreamy expression on her face. 'I love Rick to bits, but being married doesn't make me blind and Gregorio is something else.'

Yes, he was. But quite what that something else was Lia had no idea.

She knew she hadn't been able to stop thinking about him since she'd left his apartment late yesterday afternoon. Since she had made… Well, it hadn't quite been the walk of shame, because it hadn't mattered that the clothes she was wearing were the same ones she had worn to work that morning. But it had certainly been an embarrassing exit from the hotel after Lia had collected her coat from the staffroom. Made more so by the fact that the other receptionists had cheerfully wished her goodnight before she left—just as if it had been a normal working day at the Exemplar Hotel.

There had been nothing *normal* about yesterday as far as Lia was concerned.

The pleasurable aches and pains in her body when she'd woken up that morning had seemed to agree with that sentiment. Which was why she had suggested meeting up with Cathy at the gym after work. The two women had been using different apparatus since they'd arrived, so sitting in the adjoining bar, sipping iced water, was the first opportunity they had found actually to chat.

'I can see by the smile on your face that he's every bit as satisfying as I thought he might be.'

'Cathy!' Lia's cheeks were ablaze with revealing colour.

'Lia!' she came back teasingly. 'You never had that cat-that-got-the-cream expression on your face after spending the night with David.'

Lia sobered at the mention of her ex-fiancé. 'I saw David yesterday too.'

'What?' Cathy sat forward. 'When? Why?'

She sighed heavily. 'Gregorio told me some things about him and I wanted to know if they were true.'

'And were they?'

'Yes.' Lia had no doubt now that Gregorio's suspicions about David would prove to be correct. Or that he was right to be cautious about to what David might do once Gregorio had evidence against him.

'More secrets?' Cathy eyed her sympathetically.

Lia blinked back the tears that never seemed to be far away nowadays. 'Gregorio thinks David is responsible for my father's financial problems and subsequent heart attack. I'm inclined to agree with him.'

'Oh, Lia.' Cathy placed her hand over Lia's and gave it a squeeze. 'I'm so sorry.'

'But not surprised?' Lia quirked a rueful brow.

'Not really, no,' her friend acknowledged with a pained wince.

Lia laughed softly. 'You really will have to be more honest with me in future regarding the men I date!'

'Gregorio has my full approval,' Cathy supplied instantly.

He had Lia's full approval too. But that didn't change the fact that she was just another sexual conquest to him. Unfortunately she had to accept that her emotions didn't function in the same compartmentalised way as his. She already cared more for Gregorio than she should, and she didn't need to have her heart broken for a second time in a matter of months.

Had David's desertion broken her heart?

If Lia was honest, the answer was no. It had hurt that he had ended their engagement so abruptly after her father's death, but she hadn't been heartbroken in the way she would be if she allowed her emotions to become fully engaged where Gregorio was concerned.

If they weren't already...

'I was wondering when you were going to arrive home.'

Lia stiffened as she stepped out of the lift and saw David standing in the hallway, directly outside her apartment. 'How did you get in here?'

There was no reception at this small apartment complex, but it did have a key-coded panel outside the front door, and a security number that had to be logged in before the door could be opened.

She had also left Raphael, her protector for the day, sitting outside in his SUV on the other side of that locked door.

David gave an unconcerned shrug. 'I told one of the other tenants I was a new neighbour and I'd forgotten the door code. She was only too happy to let me inside.'

Lia was pretty sure there had been a lot of David's false charm involved in that conversation. Although she really would have to introduce herself properly to the other tenants, so that they knew exactly who their new neighbour was in future. They also needed to be more cautious about letting unknown people into the building.

In the meantime, she had to deal with David's unwanted presence. 'How did you find out where I'm living now?' she demanded as she walked down the hallway.

He shrugged. 'It wasn't that difficult. A friend of a friend who works for the telephone company.'

Lia eyed him warily. 'Why are you here?' He was dressed casually, in an open-necked pale blue polo shirt and designer label jeans, so he had obviously been home and changed after work before coming here.

He gave her one of his most charming smiles.

'I felt we parted badly yesterday, and I wanted to put things right between us.'

'Really?' She quirked a sceptical brow.

'Yes, really.'

The smile stayed firmly in place, but Lia knew David well enough to realise it hadn't reached his eyes.

'You said some unsettling things to me yesterday, and I wanted to set the record straight.'

Lia thought saying *really* again might be a little too much. 'That's no longer necessary,' she said.

He tensed. 'Oh?'

'I think we both know the truth, David. Which means we have nothing more to say to each other.'

'You aren't being very friendly.'

She snorted. 'Do I have reason to be?'

'We were engaged...'

'*Were engaged* being the appropriate phrase.'

'Look, I know I let you down when you needed me to be strong for you. I made a mistake, okay?' His smile became ingratiating. 'I obviously don't handle sudden death well—'

'I will *not* discuss my father with you,' Lia

snapped. *'Ever,'* she added vehemently. 'Now, I would like you to leave.'

'I just want to talk to you, Lia,' he cajoled. 'I've missed you.'

'Oh, please!' She glared her disgust. 'I realise now how completely naïve I was until a few months ago. Maybe I was just too busy being "the privileged daughter of the wealthy and powerful Jacob Fairbanks",' she said, repeating his insult of yesterday. 'If I hadn't been then perhaps I would have seen through you much sooner.'

'This isn't like you, Lia…'

David had returned to the condescending voice that was really starting to grate on Lia.

'You don't talk like this. I can only conclude that it's the influence of de la Cruz.' He gave a shake of his head. 'What on earth are you doing with a man like that anyway? He's a womaniser—and a corporate shark of the worst kind.'

'He's a more honourable man than you'll *ever* be!'

Lia knew that was the truth. In all his dealings with her Gregorio had been nothing but honest.

Even when the two of them had spent the afternoon in bed together Gregorio hadn't made any false declarations or promises—before or after.

'Now, I really want you to leave, David.' She searched agitatedly through her shoulder bag for her door key.

'What if I don't want to?'

Lia looked up sharply, butterflies fluttering in her stomach as she realised that David had moved and was now standing much too close to her in the hallway. Uncomfortably so. There was no charm nor an ingratiating smile on his face now.

'One of Gregorio's men is sitting in his car outside this building,' she challenged tensely.

David raised is brows. 'He has men watching you?'

'Protecting me, yes.'

'Protecting you from whom? *Me?*' David questioned when Lia gave him a pointed glance. 'You never used to be paranoid, Lia,' he scorned.

'I never *used to be* a lot of things that I am now.'

'So I've noticed. And not all of those changes

are for the better,' David assured her. 'But de la Cruz and his men aren't here. There's just the two of us.'

Lia was aware of that. Very much so. And she didn't like it one little bit. Didn't trust or like *David* one little bit.

'I said I want you to leave,' she repeated through gritted teeth.

'Wouldn't you like to know what *really* happened the night your father died?'

'What?' Lia gasped as she stared at him with wide eyes.

David returned her gaze challengingly. 'I said—'

'I heard you,' she dismissed agitatedly. 'What I want is an explanation of what you meant.'

He shrugged. 'I was with your father when he died.'

'I… But… There was never any mention…' She gave a shake of her head. 'I was the one to find him—slumped over his desk in the morning.'

'Our meeting was lawyer/client confidential.'

David shrugged. 'When he suddenly collapsed... Well, as I said, I don't handle sudden death well.'

'He had a heart attack in front of you and you just left him there to die?' Lia reached out to place her palm on the wall for support as she felt herself sway.

'He died almost instantly.' David's mouth was tight. 'There was nothing anyone could have done.'

'You don't know that!' Lia stared at him incredulously. 'You all but *killed* him!'

'Your father died of a heart attack,' he maintained evenly.

'But heart attacks are usually brought on by stress or shock. Did you do or say something to cause his heart attack?' Lia was having difficulty keeping down the waves of nausea churning in her stomach.

'Invite me in and I'll tell you exactly what happened.'

Lia didn't like the smug expression on David's face. Smugness caused by the fact that he knew she would want to know exactly what had happened the night her father died. That she *needed* to know.

But to do that David had said she must invite him in to her apartment.

Did she dare to be alone with him in there?

CHAPTER TEN

GREGORIO TRULY BELIEVED what he had told Lia: a man could no longer call himself a man if he ever raised his hand in anger to a woman. But right now he was very angry. With a red-hot, blinding anger.

Which meant he would have to punch a wall or something to alleviate his tension before seeing Lia. Or he could just punch David Richardson in his too-handsome face and kill two birds with one stone—or one punch.

But for now Gregorio had to concentrate on driving to Lia's apartment so that he arrived in one piece.

He had deliberately avoided the reception area of the hotel today. Had avoided Lia. She had made it clear yesterday that she didn't want to continue seeing him.

That was about to change—whether Lia liked it or not.

Raphael had telephoned him just fifteen minutes ago to report that as a routine precaution he had checked all the numberplates and owners of the cars parked in the street where Lia's apartment was located. He had found Richardson's sports car parked at the other end of the street, neatly—deliberately?—hidden between two SUVs.

Gregorio had left his hotel suite in such a hurry he had still been talking to Raphael on his cell phone when he'd stepped into the lift and impatiently punched the button for the basement car park.

If Lia had invited Richardson to her apartment, against all Gregorio's advice for her to stay away from the man...

The thought had Gregorio pressing his foot down hard on the accelerator, his expression grim.

'I'm still waiting,' Lia challenged as David stood unmoving and silent in the sitting room of her apartment.

A mocking smile tilted his lips. 'This place is a bit of a come-down for you, isn't it?'

Her gaze remained fixed on him. 'I like it.'

And she did. The apartment was compact and easy to keep clean. It was also her first very own space. She had enjoyed living with her father, but there had been a formality to it, with meals served at set times and an army of staff to cook for them and clean the house. And consequently very little privacy. Here she could do exactly as she pleased, when she pleased—including eating what and when she wanted. In the nude if she so chose.

'If you say so,' David derided sceptically.

'Well?' Lia's impatience deepened.

'Aren't you going to offer me a coffee or something?' He made himself comfortable on the sofa. 'No.'

He chuckled. 'I think I like this new, outspoken Lia after all. *Very* sexy.' His gaze ran slowly over her, from her head to her toes and back again.

Her hands clenched at her sides. 'Will you just tell me what happened the night my father died?'

David's expression became guarded. 'He invited me over. We talked. He had a heart attack. I left.'

Anger welled up, strong and unstoppable. 'You already told me that much in the hallway.'

Had her father *known* David was responsible for the missing money? Had he confronted the other man and then David had simply let her father die when he collapsed?

Why hadn't her father confided in *her*?

The answer came to Lia so suddenly and with such force she almost bent over from the pain.

David had been her fiancé. The man her father had believed she loved and intended to marry. At the time she had believed that too. She had no doubt her father had loved her enough to want to protect her from knowing the truth about her future husband.

'My father confronted you about the embezzlement of Fairbanks Industries funds.' It wasn't a question but a statement.

David's mouth twisted derisively. 'He said that

if I returned the money then no one else needed to know what I'd done.'

'But you no longer have the money, do you?'

'Not all of it, no.'

'Because you're addicted to gambling.' Lia looked at him with disgust.

'I'm not addicted!' There was an ugly expression on David's face. 'I just enjoy the thrill…the excitement.'

Addiction.

'Can't you see how it's ruining your life?' Lia frowned. 'How it's turned you into a man who steals from his clients to feed his addiction?'

'You sound just like your father,' David scorned. 'He said if I returned the money no one else need ever know about it and the two of us could live happily ever after. He withdrew from the de la Cruz negotiations to give me time to make the adjustments.'

Which proved Gregorio had been telling the truth when he'd told Lia her father had been the one to withdraw from the negotiations with De la Cruz Industries, even though the sale of the company would have saved her father and the people who worked for him.

Because he had hoped to resolve the situation of David's embezzlement from the company without anyone being any the wiser. Certainly without Lia knowing what David had done.

My father confronted David alone that evening for the same reason—because he wanted to avoid hurting me.

And David—thief, liar and manipulator that he undoubtedly was—had no doubt used her in the same way to try and blackmail her father into silence. The strain had finally proved too much for her father and he'd had a heart attack.

Lia hadn't been in her father's study that evening, nor had she heard any of the conversation between the two men, but she knew with certainty that that was exactly what had happened.

'Get out,' she told David coldly.

His brows rose. 'We haven't finished talking yet.'

'Oh, we've finished,' Lia assured him evenly. 'We're *way* beyond finished,' she added vehemently. 'My father acted the way he did out of love for me, and now I'm going to do exactly the same out of my love for him. I am going to ruin you, David, as you ruined and eventually killed my father. I'll expose you for the cheat and a liar you really are— Take your hand off me!' she protested as David stood and moved across the room so quickly she was unable to avoid his painful grasp about her wrist.

Instead of releasing her David twisted her arm and held it at a painful level against her back, stepping behind her and bringing himself nauseatingly close to her.

'I don't think so,' he murmured viciously as he bent his head close to her ear. 'Why don't you just agree to be a good girl, hmm? Otherwise...'

'Otherwise?' she echoed sharply.

He shrugged. 'Well, you're grieving for your father... Not adapting well to your change of circumstances. People would understand if you were to take a bottle of pills and just fall asleep...'

'You're insane!' Lia truly believed it at that

moment: no man in his right mind would threaten to kill her so cold-bloodedly.

'Desperate,' David corrected grimly. 'And you should know better than to threaten a desperate man, Lia.'

Gregorio had tried to warn her. *Had* warned her. Lia just hadn't listened.

Gregorio...

'You would never get away with killing me,' she warned him as she struggled and failed to release herself from David's painful grip. 'Gregorio would know I hadn't killed myself, and he would hound you until he caught you.'

'Wouldn't change the fact you were dead,' David reasoned.

There was no arguing with that logic.

Lia let out a scream as David suddenly twisted her arm so viciously she thought she was going to pass out from the pain.

'Stop fighting me and I'll stop hurting you,' he ground out harshly.

Lia ceased her struggles. She slumped weakly forward the moment David reduced that painful pressure.

* * *

Gregorio tensed in the hallway when he heard Lia scream inside the apartment, not hesitating for so much as a second before he raised his booted foot and kicked the apartment door open.

He stepped through the flying wood splinters from where the lock had been detached from the doorframe and carried on down the hallway, his eyes narrowing as he took in the scene in front of him.

David Richardson stood behind Lia, one of his arms about her waist as he held her against him, his face buried in her hair, his lips against her throat.

Had Gregorio imagined that scream?

Or perhaps the reason for it…?

He knew from personal experience that Lia was a passionate lover. She was also a noisy one. She had screamed several times when they were in bed together yesterday afternoon. Usually when she had an orgasm…

Richardson and Lia were both still fully dressed. But, again, that was no guarantee that

Lia's scream hadn't been a pleasurable one: she'd still been wearing all her clothes the first time she'd had an orgasm in his arms. Had he interrupted Richardson while he was pleasuring Lia?

Gregorio returned his narrowed gaze to Lia's face. The wide and startled eyes. The pale cheeks. The trembling lips.

The pale cheeks...

Lia's face was always flushed with pleasure when she orgasmed with him. Her eyes would glow. Her lips would be a deep rose colour.

He took in her body language, noting her tension and the fact that one of her arms was behind her back. Held there by Richardson.

Gregorio's jaw tensed. 'Let her go, Richardson.'

The other man's gaze was insolent as he looked at Gregorio over Lia's shoulder. 'She likes it here. Don't you?' he prompted Lia confidently as his arm tightened about her waist.

'I—' Lia broke off with an indrawn hiss as David gave her arm another painful twist.

She had been completely shocked when the door to her apartment had been kicked or shouldered open—so savagely the lock had come out of the doorframe, wood splintering everywhere, the door itself crashing into the wall behind.

And she had never been more pleased to see Gregorio as he stepped through that ruined doorway, looking for all the world like a dark avenging angel in a black T-shirt, black jeans and heavy black boots, the darkness of hair tousled into disarray.

She had no idea what he was doing here after the way they had parted yesterday—she was just grateful that he *was* there.

At least she would be if David hadn't given her arm that warning and very painful twist.

It was a threat that he intended to hurt her more than he already was if she attempted to alert Gregorio to the fact she was being held against her will.

To hell with that!

'He has my arm twisted behind my back—'

Lia broke off with an agonised yelp of pain as David jerked her arm up even further, the movement accompanied by a snapping sound.

Pain such as Lia had never known before radiated from her arm to the rest of her body. Black spots danced on the edge of her vision as she was thrust forward towards Gregorio, and then the blackness became all-consuming...

'Gently,' Gregorio warned softly as Raphael lifted a still unconscious Lia into his waiting arms where he sat in the back of the SUV.

The other man closed the door and got in behind the wheel to drive them to the hospital.

It was probably as well Lia was still unconscious, because Gregorio had no doubt that her arm was broken. He had heard the distinctive sound of bone cracking as Richardson had pushed her towards him.

Gregorio's arms had moved up and caught her instinctively. All of his attention had been centred on Lia as she'd fainted in his arms—probably from the added pain he had caused by catching her as she fell.

By the time Gregorio had lifted and cradled Lia carefully in his arms, and then looked around, Richardson had gone.

Gregorio had wasted precious more seconds placing Lia gently down on the sofa, before taking out his cell phone and calling down to Raphael. The bodyguard had reported that Richardson had left the building and already driven away. Not Raphael's fault: he couldn't possibly have known that Richardson was fleeing the building rather than just leaving because Gregorio had arrived.

It didn't matter. Gregorio would find Richardson—wherever he ran to. There wasn't a place on this earth where the other man would be safe from Gregorio's wrath for his having dared to physically harm Lia.

In the meantime they had to get Lia to hospital as quickly as possible. Her broken arm needed to be reset and immobilised.

And Gregorio knew her well enough to know she was going to be one seriously angry Lia when she regained consciousness.

The voices were fading in and out of Lia's consciousness, and the pain in her arm was making it impossible for her to make any sense of what was being said.

But she did recognise the three voices speaking. Cathy. Rick. And Gregorio.

Memory came rushing back to her.

David waiting for her outside her apartment… His threats…

Gregorio's unexpected and physically violent arrival…

The snapping sound in her arm as David had pushed her away from him.

The pain.

Blackness.

And then the pain again, when she'd woken up in what she presumed was the A&E department at the local hospital, having her arm X-rayed. Despite the painkillers she had been given, she had passed out again when they'd reset the broken bone.

And throughout all that Gregorio had been at her side. Not speaking. Just *there*. His face had been set in grimly austere lines. The only words he'd spoken had been to the doctor as the other man had reset her arm. Before she'd blacked out again.

She had no idea when Cathy and Rick had arrived, but she realised Gregorio must have called them. There was no other way they could have known she was at the hospital.

Talking of which…

She opened her eyes to look at the three people sitting beside the gurney she was lying on, obviously all waiting for her to wake up. She seemed to be in some sort of curtained-off area—probably still in A&E. The cast felt like a heavy weight on her left arm.

'At last the lady awakens.' Cathy beamed her pleasure.

'Thank goodness.' Rick heaved a sigh of relief. 'You had us worried for a while there, Lia.'

Only Gregorio remained silent, and a quick glance in his direction showed her that his expression was as grim as it had been earlier, his eyes a glittering black.

Lia turned away to moisten her lips before speaking. 'Can I go home now?'

'Of course.'

'Yes.'

'No!'

She winced as all three of them answered her at once. 'Conflicting answers there, guys.'

'You *can* go home…' Cathy shot Gregorio a puzzled glance—his had been the negative answer.

'But you aren't going to.' He spoke up firmly. 'Not to your own apartment, anyway.' He stood up restlessly and began to pace the confined area behind the curtains. 'I have arranged for the lock to be repaired, but Richardson is still out there somewhere,' he added grimly.

A nerve pulsed in Lia cheek before she spoke quietly. 'He was threatening to kill me and make it look like suicide before you arrived,' she told Gregorio.

'God, no…' Cathy gasped.

'Bastard!' Rick muttered furiously.

Lia moistened the dryness of her lips. 'I don't think he would have done it— Okay, maybe he would,' she conceded heavily when Cathy gave a sceptical snort.

The murderous rage Gregorio had been holding in check for the past two hours threatened to overflow like molten lava from the top of a volcano.

If he could have got hold of Richardson during the past two hours…!

He had debated long and hard as to whether or not to call the police immediately in regard to Richardson's attack on Lia. He had finally decided not to do so—not this evening, at least. He would call the police once he had Lia safe. They would add assault to the rest of the charges he was going to ask the police to bring against David Richardson once they caught him.

Raphael and Silvio were out looking for the other man now, but they had already reported back that Richardson wasn't at his apartment or his parents' house. Considering the amount of money the other man had embezzled from Fairbanks Industries, there was every possibility he had decided to leave the country. Richardson had to know that, having hurt Lia in front of Gregorio, he would now be being hunted.

Gregorio had no intention of stopping that search until he had found the other man and eliminated any further danger to Lia.

'You will stay at the hotel with me,' he stated. He couldn't concentrate his attention on the search for Richardson without knowing that Lia was completely safe.

'Oh, I'm sure there's no need—'

'We'd be more than happy—'

'There will be no discussion on the subject. Lia is coming back to the hotel with me.' Gregorio spoke over the protests of both Lia and Cathy. 'She will be safer there,' he said more gently to Cathy.

Lia inwardly questioned whether she *would* be safer at the hotel.

With Gregorio.

Alone with him day and night in that sumptuous hotel suite.

Not that she was in any condition for a seduction, and nor had Gregorio shown any signs of wanting to seduce her, but even so…

She wasn't comfortable with the idea of staying with him.

'You and Rick both have jobs to go to.' Gregorio continued to talk to Cathy in that soothing tone. 'I can work from my hotel suite, and very often do. Lia will not be left alone at any time until Richardson has been apprehended.'

Oh, great—now she was going to have a babysitter—no doubt Silvio or Raphael—whenever Gregorio had to go out.

'I'd really rather not—'

'The matter is settled,' Gregorio rasped, and those glittering black eyes were challenging as he looked at her.

When Gregorio announced that a matter was settled it was well and truly settled, Lia acknowledged a few minutes later as she sat beside him in the back of the SUV while Silvio drove them back to the hotel.

She couldn't deny there was a certain logic to her staying with Gregorio. David was obviously more dangerous than she had realised, and she didn't doubt his threat to kill her had been very real. The penthouse floor of the Exemplar Hotel was completely private to Gregorio, and he already had his own security team in place.

Besides, she accepted that going back to her apartment was a bad idea. Even though Gregorio had already had the lock and the door repaired, she didn't trust David any more.

She certainly didn't want to put Cathy and Rick in any danger by accepting their offer to stay with them.

Lia had never thought she would say it—even think it—but Gregorio's hotel suite *was* the safest place for her to stay right now.

CHAPTER ELEVEN

'YOU ARE GOING to need help undressing, and I will put something waterproof over the cast on your arm before you have a shower,' Gregorio informed her evenly as he unpacked the bag of Lia's clothes and toiletries that Cathy and Rick had just collected and brought over from Lia's apartment.

Lia gave a grimace as she sat on the side of the bed in what had turned out to be one of six spare bedrooms in Gregorio's suite. Not that she had expected to be invited to share Gregorio's bed-room, but this impersonal guest room told her exactly the place she occupied in his life.

She really hadn't thought things through enough when she had accepted that Gregorio's suite was the safest and best place for her to be right now. She hadn't thought about where she would actually sleep. Nor taken into account the mechanics of not being able to move her right arm properly, or the fact that she was going to be encumbered with a heavy plaster cast for the next six weeks, and a sling for two of them.

Which meant she couldn't undress herself without assistance, and showering was going to be a big problem. She would probably need to have her food cut up into tiny pieces too, so she could eat with one hand.

But right now her thoughts sounded like those of a whiny, ungrateful brat. 'I'll take a bath instead of a shower,' she announced brightly. 'And I'm sure I'll be able to take my own clothes off.'

She knew the strong painkillers she had been given at the hospital were preventing her from feeling the worst of the pain. Luckily she had been prescribed a whole plastic container full of them!

Gregorio arched a dark brow. 'I have already seen you naked, Lia…'

She shot him an irritated scowl. 'Not under these circumstances, you haven't!' She sighed as she realised she sounded ungrateful. 'I'm sorry, Gregorio. I haven't even thanked you yet for coming to my rescue earlier.'

'Luckily Raphael recognised Richardson's car and called me immediately.' Gregorio leaned back against the tall chest of drawers he had placed her clothes in, arms folded across his chest, his expression unreadable. 'What exactly did Richardson threaten to do to you?'

Lia wasn't fooled for a moment by his relaxed posture, or the mildness of his tone. 'I'm sure he wouldn't really have— No, I'm not.' She admitted with a grimace. 'He was… I had no idea he could be like that. I owe you an apology, Gregorio. Another one. Everything you said about David is true.'

'He is responsible for embezzling the money from your father's company?'

'Oh, yes.'

'He admitted this to you?'

'Amongst other things.'

She related everything David had said to her earlier that evening.

'He was *with* your father the night he died…?' Gregorio frowned.

Lia closed her eyes briefly before opening them again. 'He said there was nothing to be done. That my father died almost instantly. But—' She broke off, unable to say anything more on the subject without breaking down.

'But,' Gregorio acknowledged harshly, 'you think he is responsible for killing your father?'

'Only indirectly—in as much as he caused my father so much distress it brought on the heart attack.'

His mouth thinned. 'I will find him, Lia. No matter what rock Richardson hides under, I *will* find him.'

'I know you will.' She nodded. 'Would you mind very much if I don't take a bath or a shower tonight? I'm tired and aching and I just want to go to sleep.'

'Of course. Whatever you are comfortable with,' Gregorio reassured her as he straightened away from the chest of drawers and crossed the bedroom to her side. 'But I *am* going to help you undress.'

Lia knew that tone only too well: it was one that told her Gregorio wasn't going to be talked out of doing exactly what he said he would. And there was no arguing with the fact that he *had* already seen her naked.

'Did Cathy pack something for me to sleep in?' She stood up—only to have Gregorio reach out and grasp her uninjured arm to steady her as she tilted to one side. It was ridiculous how a little thing like a plaster cast and a sling could affect her balance.

'Something that looks like an oversized T-shirt…?'

'That's it, yes.'

Lia almost laughed at the look of disgust on Gregorio's face. No doubt he was used to the women in his life wearing silk and satin to bed— if they bothered to wear anything at all. Even when she'd been able to afford those things Lia had always preferred practicality and warmth in bed over appearing sexy.

'Thank you for calling Cathy and Rick for me earlier. I— They're the closest thing to family I have.'

'I am aware of that.' Gregorio spoke softly. 'And I have already left instructions that they are to be admitted at any time.'

'Thank you.'

He gave a rueful smile. 'You are very polite this evening.'

'About time, hmm?'

Gregorio shrugged. 'You felt you had good reason to be...less than polite to me before.'

'And I was wrong.' She sighed. 'About everything.'

'Do not upset yourself. You know the truth now, and that is the important thing.'

It was. And yet...

She didn't like it that Gregorio was treating her with the polite distance of a concerned acquaintance, rather than a lover. Not that she didn't fully deserve it, but Lia missed the intensity of passion radiating from him. That had never been far from the surface when the two of them had been together in the past.

She drew in a shaky breath. 'Let's get this over with, shall we?'

'Of course.'

Gregorio forced himself to remain detached and impersonal as he aided Lia in removing her clothes. He had never acted as nursemaid to anyone before—let alone a woman he had been in bed with all yesterday afternoon. But how difficult could it be?

More difficult that he had imagined once he had removed Lia's jacket, blouse and bra. Which had proved easy enough once he had removed the sling.

The physical removing of Lia's clothes wasn't the problem. It was being this close to her when she was completely naked from the waist up, the fullness of her nipples just a tempting breath away. That was enough to tax the restraint of any man—least of all one who had already enjoyed having those succulent nipples in his mouth.

Gregorio attempted to remove temptation by

taking the long red T-shirt from the chest of drawers and quickly putting it on Lia before re-fastening the sling. The nightshirt covered her to mid-thigh.

He drew in a deep, controlling breath as he un-zipped and removed her skirt, but his resolve to remain detached was shaken again as he looked at her wearing sexy panties, suspenders and stockings.

He could *do* this, damn it. He wasn't an ani-mal or a callow youth. He was a man of sophis-tication and experience. He shouldn't be aroused just by looking at an injured woman dressed in an unbecoming red nightshirt—even if she *was* also wearing sexy suspenders.

Except he was.

Thank goodness the restrictive material of his jeans prevented that arousal from being too ob-vious.

'Gregorio…?'

His distraction obviously wasn't quite so easy to hide!

He dealt with the rest of Lia's clothing with the

minimum of contact with the heat of her silky skin, breathing a sigh of relief once he had her safely tucked beneath the bedcovers and could straighten and move away from the bed.

Lia looked…fragile. Her hair was a silky auburn cloud on the white pillow behind her, and her face was almost as pale. The outline of her body was slender beneath the duvet.

But it wasn't just a physical fragility. Lia's eyes were a smoky and unfocused grey, with dark shadows beneath them. No doubt some of that had been caused by the agony of having her arm broken, along with the medication she had been given to relieve the pain. But Gregorio had a feeling it was also an outward show of the turmoil of emotions she had to be feeling inside.

It must have been a shock when Richardson had attacked and threatened her in that way: the animal had broken her arm, damn it. She had intended marrying Richardson once—would no doubt have done so if her father hadn't died and Richardson hadn't revealed his true colours by breaking their engagement.

As far as Gregorio was concerned Lia had escaped being married to a man who one day would have become an abusive husband.

Lia, on the other hand, must feel not only foolish for ever having been taken in by Richardson, but also disillusioned with the whole concept of falling in love.

'Try to get some sleep.' Gregorio's voice sounded harsher than he'd intended, and he made a concerted effort to control his anger. It was Richardson he was angry with, not Lia. 'I will leave the door open, and I'll be in my office or my bedroom if you need anything.'

'Thank you.' The heaviness of her lids was already making them close.

Gregorio hesitated at the door. 'Would you like the light left on or turned off?'

'On!' She half sat up again in the bed. 'Off.' She grimaced as she sank back against the pillows. 'I don't know...' She groaned.

'We will compromise.' He nodded. 'I'll leave the door open and the light on in the hallway, okay?'

'Okay…' She sighed wearily.

Gregorio adjusted the lighting before quietly leaving the bedroom. As promised, he left the door open.

Only once he had reached the sanctuary of his office did he release the anger that had been building and building inside him by slamming his fist against the door. It hurt him more than it hurt the wooden door, but he needed the release, the physical pain, after remaining calm for Lia's sake for so long.

He wanted to hurt someone. And that someone was David Richardson. Because Lia was suffering the emotional and physical repercussions of the other man's abuse.

He had known she was suffering physically, but her emotional trauma had shown itself in her immediate reaction to the thought of being left alone in the darkness of the bedroom. Lia was frightened, but too determined to appear strong to want Gregorio to see that fear. He had seen it anyway.

His expression was grim as he flexed his bruised

knuckles before pouring himself a glass of brandy, carrying the glass across the room to sit in the chair behind his desk.

He swung his booted feet up to rest on the edge of the desk and turned his head to stare out of the window at the night-time skyline. Was Richardson still out there in the city somewhere, hiding? Or had he already left the country? Not that it mattered, because Gregorio wouldn't give up the search—no matter how far Richardson had run.

Gregorio had no idea how long he sat there, sipping brandy and staring sightlessly out of the window, totally aware of Lia just feet away, almost naked in bed. He felt a certain relief when his cell phone vibrated in his jeans pocket and interrupted his reverie. His thoughts had been going round and round in ever decreasing circles, none of them pleasant.

He took out his cell phone and checked the caller ID before taking the call. 'Sebastien,' he greeted his brother tersely.

'Who's annoyed you *now*?' Sebastien didn't waste any time on pleasantries.

'It is too long and too complicated a story to tell.'

'Try…' his brother drawled.

Gregorio gave him a condensed—and censored—version of the events of the past week.

The three brothers had always been close, having shared a common enemy: their father's sometimes overbearing machismo. As adults the siblings had also become friends, and Sebastien was the closest thing Gregorio had to a confidant.

'So Jacob Fairbanks's daughter—Lia—is there with you now, in your hotel suite?' Sebastien prompted speculatively.

'She is asleep in one of the guest rooms, yes,' Gregorio stated. 'She has a cast on her broken arm and no particular liking for *me*,' he added firmly. 'Sebastien…?' he prompted at his brother's continued silence.

'Just give me a second while I choose my words carefully, Rio…' Sebastien spoke slowly. 'Our proposed deal with Jacob Fairbanks was called off months ago, and you told me she slapped you on the face at his funeral—so what is Lia Fairbanks doing in your life *now*?'

Trust Sebastien to go straight to the heart of the matter.

The heart...?

Gregorio had physically wanted Lia from the moment he saw her in that restaurant four months ago. This past week he had come to know the Lia behind that physical beauty. To like her. For her strength. Her principles. Her loyalty—even if it occasionally proved to be misplaced!—and her love for her father and her friends. Her work ethic was also exemplary: Michael Harrington had already told Gregorio he believed Lia would become one of their most competent receptionists.

Had Gregorio come to *like* her or to *love* her?

Until this mess was sorted out and Lia was safe he had no intention of delving too deeply into what his feelings for her might be.

'Taking a long time to answer, there, Rio,' Sebastien mocked.

'You are my brother—not my conscience!'

Sebastien chuckled. 'And...?'

'I feel a sense of obligation to ensure Lia's safety,' Gregorio answered him carefully.

'Why?'

'Because she is— Sebastien, her father—the only parent she had—is dead. David Richardson, her ex-fiancé, deserted her when she most needed him. He has now admitted to embezzling from her father's company, and that is the reason Jacob called off his deal with us. Richardson left Lia alone until he knew the two of us were…acquainted…' He substituted the word he had intended using. One afternoon in bed together did not make him and Lia lovers, and she had made it clear she didn't intend to repeat the experience. 'And then he attacked her, threatened her. He broke her *arm*, dammit!'

'And you feel responsible for her?'

'Yes, I feel responsible for her,' he repeated evenly.

Lia, standing outside in the hallway, overhearing Gregorio's side of the conversation with his brother, hadn't realised how much hearing those words spoken out loud would hurt until Gregorio said them. It was one thing to *think* that was what had motivated Gregorio's continued interest in her—another entirely to hear him state as much to his brother.

She had slept for a couple of hours, only to wake up suddenly, totally disorientated until she remembered where she was and why. Once awake she had realised how thirsty she was, and had got out of bed, quietly leaving the bedroom so as not to disturb Gregorio on her way to the kitchen for a glass of water.

She hadn't meant to eavesdrop on his telephone conversation with his brother, but once she'd heard her name mentioned she hadn't been able to walk away either.

Gregorio had saved her again this evening. He was always saving her from one disaster or another.

Because he feels responsible for me.

Well, that had to change. Maybe not right now, because it was far too late for her even to think of moving out of the hotel and finding somewhere else to stay tonight, and she was determined not to involve Cathy and Rick in any further acts of violence from David. But tomorrow, when she was feeling stronger and able to make other arrangements, she was going to stop being a burden on Gregorio and take control of her own life—as she had said she was going to.

Tomorrow.

'Wake up, Lia! It is not real, *bella*, only a nightmare. *Lia?*' Gregorio prompted more firmly as she continued to scream, the tears streaming from her closed eyes and down her cheeks as she fought off his attempts to take her in his arms.

Gregorio had drunk several more glasses of brandy before going to bed, knowing he was going to need the relaxant if he stood any chance of sleeping at all.

It had taken some time, but he had finally dozed off into a fitful slumber. Only to be woken—minutes…hours later?—by the sound of Lia screaming.

At first he had thought someone—Richardson—had managed to get past his security and Lia was being attacked. It was only once he had entered her bedroom and found her there alone, screaming as she tossed from side to side in the bed, that he realised she was obviously in the middle of some horrendous nightmare.

His efforts to calm her had so far been unsuccessful.

'Lia!' He was careful not to knock the cast on her arm as he grasped her shoulders. 'Open your eyes and look at me, Lia,' he instructed firmly.

She'd stopped screaming, at least, and her eyes were open, but her body was still being racked by intense sobs.

'It was just a nightmare…it isn't real,' he continued to soothe as he took her in his arms.

It seemed very real to Lia!

She was running, knowing that something… someone…was pursuing her. She couldn't see him when she dared to take a quick glance behind her, but she could feel him, hear him breathing—could almost *feel* that hot breath on the back of her neck. And then he was there—in front of her—not behind her at all. An indistinct dark shadow and yet she knew it was a man. Knew it was David. And he wanted to kill her.

'You are safe now, Lia.' Gregorio held her tightly. 'No one will harm you while I am here. I promise you.'

But he wouldn't always be there, would he? She was just a woman Gregorio felt a fleeting obligation to protect. Because she was alone in the world and she needed his help. He didn't *really* care about her. They'd had sex yesterday afternoon, and that was the reason he probably felt even this much obligation. Right now he was probably regretting that he had ever shown an interest in her at all. She brought too much baggage with her, and Gregorio de la Cruz wasn't interested in a woman with baggage.

'I'm okay now.' She was very aware of the fact that Gregorio wore only a pair of loose jogging trousers, and his chest was completely bare. The warm and muscular chest he was holding her against... 'I'm sorry if I disturbed you.' His half-nakedness was certainly disturbing *her*! 'I'll be fine now.'

She kept her gaze lowered as she attempted to

pull away. Gregorio's arms only tightened in reaction.

'Lia, look at me.'

She didn't want to look at him. At any part of him. Bad enough that her hand that wasn't restricted by the sling was now pressed against Gregorio's chest, that his flesh was warm and sensual to the touch.

'Lia?'

She glanced up at Gregorio's face and then quickly down again. His hair was tousled from sleep, his eyes black, and dark stubble lined his jaw. He looked incredibly sexy. And he smelt edible. A cross between the lingering aroma of that expensive cologne he wore and something else—a male musk that was uniquely Gregorio.

She felt her body's response to all that overwhelming male lushness.

Gregorio simply felt an obligation to look out for her, Lia firmly reminded herself. That was the only reason he had been around this past couple of months.

And in return she had slapped him at her father's funeral, been incredibly rude to him before asking him to leave her apartment, and then yesterday—yesterday she had told him she didn't want him. That she never wanted to go to bed with him again.

Liar, liar, pants on fire.

She could lie to Gregorio, but there was no longer any chance of lying to herself.

She was in love with Gregorio.

Not infatuated, not sexually enthralled by him—although she was that too!—but one hundred per cent in love with him.

He was everything a man should be. Honourable. Truthful. Protective of those he deemed weaker than himself. A man Lia knew instinctively her father had liked as well as respected. And the reason she knew that was because her father had recognised those traits in Gregorio.

In the same way her father had known that David was none of those things. If he had lived, would her father have told her the truth about David? Or would he have continued to lie and cover up for the younger man because he wouldn't have wanted to hurt Lia by exposing the true nature of the man she loved?

Lia hoped it would have been the former, and that her father would have realised she was strong enough to accept the truth.

None of which changed the fact that she had now fallen deeply in love with a man who was never going to want her as more than a friend with benefits.

'I'll be fine now,' Lia assured Gregorio lightly as she pulled out of his arms. 'Please go back to bed. *Please.*'

'Sure?' He studied her closely.

'Sure.' She nodded, keeping that bright look on her face until Gregorio had left the bedroom.

Which was when Lia closed her eyes and allowed hot tears to fall down her cheeks.

CHAPTER TWELVE

'MIGHT I ASK what you are doing here, Sebastien?'

Gregorio's brother had arrived at the hotel just minutes ago. Considering it was only eight o'clock in the morning, Sebastien had to have flown here in the second company jet overnight from New York. Almost immediately after the two men had concluded their telephone conversation the night before, in fact.

His brother stepped back from their brotherly hug. 'You didn't sound at all yourself when we spoke on the phone last night, Rio.'

He arched dark and sceptical brows. 'And that was reason enough for you to immediately fly to London?'

Sebastien gave him a boyish grin. 'That, and I wanted to see Lia Fairbanks for myself.'

Gregorio tensed. 'Why?'

Sebastien's grin grew even wider. 'I wanted to meet the woman who has my big brother so tied up in knots.'

'Stop talking nonsense,' Gregorio snapped. 'No doubt you would like a cup of coffee?'

He turned away to pour some of the strong brew he always made to accompany his breakfast. He had already drunk two full cups this morning, having been unable to fall asleep again after Lia's nightmare. He had wanted to stay alert in case Lia needed him again.

'No changing the subject, Rio.' Sebastien made himself comfortable at one of the high stools at the breakfast bar as he accepted the mug of coffee. 'What's so special about Lia Fairbanks?' He kept his eyes on Gregorio as he took a swallow.

Everything.

The thought had leapt unbidden into Gregorio's head, and once there he couldn't seem to dislodge it.

Lia was special. *Very* special. A woman who remained strong through adversity. Most women would have been hysterical after Richardson's attack last night, but Lia had remained calm. And this was after she had lost her father only two and a half months ago and her engagement had ended—although after the events of yesterday she was probably relieved that it had.

As for the way the two of them were in bed together...

Lia was like none of the women Gregorio had known in the past. She gave not only with her body but with all that she was. Gregorio had never known a lover like her before.

Would he ever know another lover like her again?

'Perhaps I'll know the answer to that once I've met her?' Sebastien was still eyeing him speculatively.

Gregorio felt an unaccustomed surge of possessiveness at the thought of Lia meeting Sebastien. Would she find Sebastien attractive, as so many other women did? The two brothers were very alike in looks, with their dark hair and dark eyes, and a similar build and height.

Would Lia find his brother easier to get along with than Gregorio?

That was a given. Gregorio was well aware that he lacked the charm and ease of manner Sebastien could so easily adopt if the need arose. And meeting a beautiful woman was definitely one of those occasions.

The thought of Lia gravitating towards Sebastien was enough to cause Gregorio's hand to clench at his side and his fingers to tighten about his coffee mug until the knuckles turned white.

'I'm guessing you don't like that idea.' Sebastien grinned.

Gregorio gave his brother an irritated glance. 'Do not see emotions where they do not exist.'

Sebastien openly chuckled now. 'If you don't stop gripping the handle of that mug so tightly you're going to snap it right off.'

He relaxed that grip. 'You would be better spending your time thinking of ways to help me locate David Richardson than commenting on things you know nothing about.'

'I know nothing about Richardson, either.'

Gregorio's lids narrowed on his brother. 'This situation needs to be resolved, Sebastien. Quickly.'

'But then Miss Fairbanks would move back to her own apartment.'

'Exactly.'

'Rio—'

'Why are you *really* here, Sebastien?' Gregorio looked at his brother searchingly, noting the lines beside his brother's mouth and eyes that didn't gel with his light-hearted banter. 'What's wrong?'

Sebastien sighed heavily. 'Nothing a hot and meaningless fling wouldn't cure.'

Gregorio winced. 'Do you have someone specific in mind?'

His brother grimaced. 'Maybe.'

Definitely, in Gregorio's opinion. 'Who is she?'

'Could we just concentrate on *your* problems rather than my own?' Sebastien prompted impatiently.

'This woman is a *problem*, then?'

'Monumentally so,' his brother conceded. 'But

don't worry. I'll handle it when I get back to New York.'

'Handle it or handle her?'

Sebastien gave a hard grin. 'Both.'

'I hope I'm not interrupting?'

Gregorio turned sharply at the sound of Lia's voice, a scowl darkening his brow as he saw she was only dressed in that over-large thigh-length red T-shirt, with her arm in its sling over the top of it and her hair dishevelled from sleep.

'I'm Sebastien de la Cruz.' His brother stood politely. 'I hope we didn't wake you?'

'Lia Fairbanks,' she returned stiltedly. 'And, no, you didn't wake me. I just woke up and felt in need of coffee.'

'My big brother is in charge of the coffee pot. Rio…?' he prompted as Gregorio made no move to pour a third cup.

It was the first time Lia had heard anyone address him by the affectionate diminutive; it made him seem less the powerful and arrogant Gregorio de la Cruz and more the older brother. The casual navy blue polo shirt and faded jeans he wore added to that illusion.

She hadn't been able to help overhearing at least part of Gregorio's conversation with Sebastien—again. The little she had heard made it clear Gregorio wanted her out of his hotel suite as soon as possible.

Not that it came as a surprise. She already knew Gregorio had only insisted she come here at all because of that sense of responsibility he felt towards her. Nevertheless, hearing him reiterate those feelings to his brother made it all too real.

'You are not dressed appropriately to receive visitors,' Gregorio bit out tautly. 'I suggest you return to your bedroom and put on a robe, at least.'

Lia frowned at the censure she could hear in his tone. And at the continued lack of coffee. 'I can't manage on my own.' She gave a pointed glance at the sling immobilising her arm.

'Then I will come and assist you.' Gregorio straightened. 'If you will excuse us, Sebastien?'

'Don't bother on my account.' Sebastien resumed his seat on the bar stool. 'I think you look charming just as you are. Rio has explained that your arm is broken,' he said sympathetically.

Lia was sure, from the conversation she had overheard, that Sebastien de la Cruz was well aware of exactly how she had broken her arm. Or rather, how it had been broken for her.

Now that she was no longer in excruciating pain, and the effects of the painkillers had worn off a little, she was aware of the shock of exactly what David had done to her. Of what else he had threatened to do to her if she didn't back off.

She really hadn't known the true David at all until last night.

She gave a grimace in answer to Sebastien's comment. 'It could have been worse.'

'So I understand.' He nodded. 'I'm sorry you've had to go through this.'

'The princess had to be woken by the frog some time. It's what my father called me,' she explained emotionally as both men looked at her. 'His princess.'

A princess he had protected from seeing or hearing any of the harsh realities of life. Until he'd died from the strain of trying to protect her from the harshest reality. Well, Lia was well and truly awake to all those realities now—she had the plaster cast on her broken arm to prove it.

'I will accompany you to your bedroom and help you into your robe,' Gregorio announced into the silence.

Lia turned her frowning attention on him. 'I haven't had any coffee yet.'

'Because I have not poured you any. Nor will I do so until you are wearing your robe.'

'I'm perfectly decent as I am.' The nightshirt covered her from her neck to a couple of inches above her knees.

'I will be the judge of that.' His mouth was thin, his dark eyes glittering.

Lia gave a squeak of protest as Gregorio grasped her shoulders and turned her in the direction of the hallway and her bedroom, walking her forward in front of him. 'I can walk unassisted!'

'Then do so.' He released her, but his presence behind her continued her impetus out of the kitchen.

'What is *wrong* with you?' Lia demanded impatiently once they were outside in the hallway.

His eyes narrowed. 'You are virtually naked in front of a complete stranger.'

'He's your *brother*, for goodness' sake.'

'And you met him for the first time five minutes ago—which makes him a stranger to you.'

'"Virtually naked" would be wearing only my underwear,' Lia defended. 'And I don't remember you complaining the last time I was in your suite dressed like that,' she challenged.

Gregorio could feel that nerve pulsing in his cheek again—a common occurrence, it seemed, when he was with this stubbornly determined woman. 'And I would not complain if you were to be dressed like that again—as long as the two of us were alone together when you were.'

'Sebastien didn't seem to mind the way I'm dressed,' she taunted.

His lids narrowed to slits. 'If you are trying to annoy me you are succeeding!'

Lia snorted. 'I obviously don't have to try very hard.'

Gregorio frowned. 'What do you mean?'

'Never mind.' She shook her head before turning to continue walking down the hallway.

Gregorio caught up with her as she reached her bedroom. 'What did you mean by that remark?' he repeated as he followed her inside.

She turned to face him. 'I'm obviously nothing more than a nuisance to you. Even more so now that your brother has arrived.'

Lia was *so* much more to Gregorio than a nuisance. More than he was prepared to admit. Even to himself.

'Well?'

He scowled his irritation. 'Do not take that aggressive tone with me!'

'Or what?'

'What is wrong with you this morning?' he snapped.

'You've refused to give me my first cup of coffee of the day.'

Gregorio drew in a deep breath in order to hold

on to his temper. 'Only until after you have put your robe on.'

'And I'm still waiting for the assistance you so gallantly offered.'

Gregorio ignored her sarcasm as he helped her to put her robe on. Lia was obviously spoiling for a fight this morning, and he wasn't about to give her one.

'Did you know that your accent gets stronger when you're angry?'

He finished tying the robe of the belt about her waist before stepping back. 'Then I must presume it is always stronger when I am with you.'

Lia arched a mocking auburn brow. 'Did you just make a joke?'

'Doubtful,' he drawled dryly.

'Irony *is* joking.'

'Then I must make jokes all the time.'

'When you're with me.' She nodded.

'When I am with anyone.'

Lia eyed him quizzically. 'You and your brother aren't much alike, are you?'

He tensed. 'In looks—'

'Oh, I wasn't talking about the way you look—that's a given,' she dismissed without further explanation. 'What is your youngest brother like?'

'Alejandro is…complicated,' he replied cautiously.

Alejandro's problems were not discussed outside the family.

'Like you, then.' Lia nodded. 'He was married, wasn't he?'

That was part of Alejandro's problem. And what did Lia mean by saying that *he* was complicated?

His life was an open book. He was a successful businessman. Wealthy. Single. He had a healthy sexual appetite, as the newspapers were so fond of reporting, and he didn't hide the fact that he had zero patience with incompetence or triviality. Or that he was bored very easily.

Something he had certainly never been when he was with Lia…

'You're taking too long to answer, which probably means you aren't going to.' Lia sighed. 'Can we go back to the kitchen now? The coffee is calling to me.'

Gregorio gave an exasperated laugh as he followed her out of the bedroom. 'You are obsessed with your morning coffee!'

'He left with a scowl on his face and returns smiling,' Sebastien observed mockingly as Lia and Gregorio entered the kitchen together. 'You're a miracle-worker, Lia.'

She grimaced. 'I think you'll find Gregorio was laughing *at* me rather than with me.'

Sebastien shrugged. 'A smile is still a smile, for whatever reason.'

'Is that such a rare occurrence?' Lia seemed to recall that Gregorio had laughed quite often when the two of them were together. When they weren't arguing or making love...

'I would say unique rather than—'

'When the two of you have quite finished discussing me as if I am not here...' Gregorio raised pointed brows as he handed Lia the mug of coffee he had just poured for her.

Oh, Lia was only too aware that Gregorio was

there. As she'd said, Sebastien was as dark and handsome as his brother. But he possessed an easy charm that was lacking in Gregorio—although, on closer inspection, the sharp intelligence in Sebastien's eyes gave the impression that that might be a veneer over a deeper, darker nature. But it was Gregorio she was constantly aware of. Every minute. Every second.

Lia chose to concentrate on drinking her coffee rather than make any reply to Gregorio's comment. Until the silence in the kitchen became uncomfortable. 'What were the two of you discussing when I came in?' Apart from the fact that Gregorio couldn't wait to move her out of his hotel suite.

'Your ex-fiancé.' Sebastien was the one to answer her.

She winced. 'I would rather not be reminded of that fact.'

'As would we all,' Gregorio put in harshly.

Lia gave him a sharp glance, knowing she deserved the admonition in his tone. Thank goodness she was no longer that naïve nincompoop who had fallen for David's charm. 'Any news on his whereabouts?'

'None,' Gregorio answered grimly. 'Lia, the police will be coming here to interview you in just under an hour—'

'The police?' she echoed sharply.

He nodded. 'We can and will find Richardson, Lia, but it's better if the police bring him to justice for the things he has done. As such, I telephoned the police and reported his attack on you last night first thing this morning. The story will be backed up by the broken door and the hospital report on your broken arm.'

She carefully placed her empty coffee mug down on the breakfast bar. 'You should have consulted me before doing that.'

'Why?'

'Why?'

'Uh-oh—I think I'll go and take a shower and grab a couple of hours' sleep, if no one minds.' Sebastien glanced between the two of them. Lia was glaring at Gregorio and he looked genuinely perplexed by her anger. 'Obviously no one is even going to notice I've gone!'

Lia waited only as long as it took for Sebastien to leave the room before answering Gregorio. 'You had no right to contact the police without talking to me first.'

'I had *every* right.' A nerve pulsed in his tightly clenched jaw. 'I should have called them last night, once we reached the hospital, but I decided to wait until today—'

'It wasn't your decision to make—'

'God knows what would have happened to you last night if I hadn't kicked open the door to your apartment!'

She was well aware of how much she owed Gregorio. 'But the *police*, Gregorio...' She groaned as she sank down onto one of the bar stools.

Gregorio frowned as he saw how pale her cheeks had become. 'Do you not see that this is the best way to put Richardson in the spotlight of the authorities? The police will want to know the motivation for his attack on you, and I will hand over to the police all the information I have gathered so far in regard to Richardson's illegal dealings with your father.'

Lia saw *Gregorio's* motivation. It had been very cleverly done.

He had taken care of two problems at the same time. He would pass on the information he had concerning Fairbanks Industries to the police and at the same time ensure that this situation ended as quickly as possible. The two of them would then be able to get on with their own respective lives.

Which was what she wanted too.

Wasn't it?

CHAPTER THIRTEEN

LIA LAY HER head back against the sofa in exhaustion after the police had asked all their questions and finally left the hotel. But she wasn't too tired to remember that she was supposed to be working today. 'I need to contact Mike Harrington to tell him I won't be in today.'

Gregorio's brow rose at hearing Lia call the hotel manager *Mike* Harrington; he had only ever known the other man by the more formal Michael. 'I have already spoken to him.'

'Why am I not surprised?' Lia muttered.

'At the time I was unsure of what time you were going to wake this morning,' he defended.

'Fair enough.' She sighed. 'I'm just wondering whose life you ran before taking over mine?'

'Lia—'

'It's okay.' She held up a defeated hand. 'I understand.'

'Understand what, exactly?'

'That the quicker this is resolved the sooner I'll be out of this suite and your life.' She stood. 'I think I'll take some more painkillers and then follow Sebastien's example of taking a nap for a couple of hours.'

She left the sitting room.

Gregorio was so stunned by her first comment that he was barely aware of the second one.

Lia believed he wanted to hasten her departure—not just from this suite but from his life. What had he ever said or done to make her think that?

His only motivation in ending this situation with Richardson was to ensure that nothing like last night ever happened again. He also wanted to clear her father's name. Again for Lia's sake, more than anyone else's.

Lia had been very defensive this morning. Spoiling for a fight. Earlier Gregorio had put it down to late reaction to the shock of Richardson's attack last night. But what if it was for another reason entirely? Her barbs and sarcasm had been directed solely at him, Gregorio now realised. Much to Gregorio's annoyance she had joked with Sebastien a couple of times this morning. Usually at Gregorio's expense. And she had been calm and polite when she answered the questions put to her by the police.

He didn't understand why. What had he and Sebastien been discussing shortly before Lia joined them in the kitchen earlier?

Damn it!

Sebastien had been teasing Gregorio about his responses to Lia, and he had reacted defensively to that teasing. Had denied that Lia had any importance in his life amongst other things. One of those things being stating his need to resolve the situation quickly and to agree that it was so that Lia could move back to her apartment.

He hadn't meant that the way it had sounded— had only been fending off Sebastien's too-personal comments.

Perhaps he shouldn't have said it? Especially in

a place where there had been a chance that Lia might overhear the comment.

Damn, damn, *damn* it.

Lia's first thought on waking up was that there was something heavy lying across her. Then she realised it had to be the unwieldy plaster cast she had on her arm.

Except… This weight felt lower down than the plaster cast. Warmer too. More flexible.

She carefully lifted the duvet so she could see what it was.

An arm.

A bare and muscular *male* arm, lightly dusted with dark hair.

An arm she easily recognised as belonging to Gregorio.

Gregorio is in bed with me!

Lia was sure he hadn't been there when she'd fallen asleep earlier, almost the instant her head had touched the pillow. She had been exhausted from talking with the police for over an hour, and then the painkillers had finally kicked in.

Gregorio must have come to her bedroom and got into the bed with her some time after that.

A part of her knew she should be annoyed, at the very least, at his having taken advantage of her sleeping. Another part of her just wanted to curl up in his arms and go back to sleep.

She also couldn't help wondering if the rest of him was as naked as his arm...

She took care not to wake Gregorio as she scooted backwards until her bottom came into contact with his groin. She was more than a little disappointed to feel the brush of denim against her skin where her nightshirt had rucked up as she'd moved about in her sleep.

'If you move back a little further you will discover that I am fully aroused.'

Lia instantly tensed at the unexpectedness of discovering that Gregorio was awake. Was it because she had woken him? Or had he already been awake when she'd been fidgeting about trying to discover what was curved about her waist? And in her careful—and obvious—efforts to discover if Gregorio was naked...?

She moistened her lips before speaking. 'What are you doing in here?'

'Until a few minutes ago I was sleeping.'

'I meant—'

'I know what you meant, Lia.' Gregorio moved up to roll her gently onto her back so that he could look at her, careful not to jar her arm. Her face had more colour than earlier, thank goodness. Her eyes no longer had that haunted look, either. 'I wanted to be here when you woke up.'

'Why?'

'Two reasons.'

'Which are?'

'Silvio contacted me shortly after you had gone to sleep. He and Raphael discovered Richardson was booked on a flight to Dubai.'

Her eyes widened. 'He was fleeing the country?'

'I believe in the beginning, with your father dead, he thought he could weather the storm and his life here in England would go on as before, with no one any the wiser as to what he had done. But—'

'But yesterday I alerted him to the fact that wasn't going to happen.' She winced. 'I'm *so* sorry, Gregorio. I just wanted him to know I wasn't as stupid as he thought I was, but all I did was give him the opportunity to leave England as soon as possible.'

'Do not feel bad about that. Richardson's response to your warning was damning in the extreme. Besides,' he added with satisfaction, 'he is now in police custody, after an anonymous phone call informing them he was booked onto the Dubai flight.'

She gave a shudder. 'He's a lawyer, Gregorio— do you think the charges against him will stick or will he manage to wriggle out of them?'

'His attack on you will certainly stick. The FSA will also be very interested in Richardson's behaviour. Especially as I have now given them all the information I have so far on his having embezzled money from Fairbanks Industries. It may take some time but, yes, I believe eventually Richardson will be made to answer for all his crimes.'

Lia gave a shaky sigh. 'I can't believe it's over.'

'In *time* it will be,' Gregorio cautioned again.

Lia had no doubt that with the powerful Gregorio de la Cruz's involvement that time would come sooner rather than later, and that David would one day end up in jail—as he fully deserved to.

'You said there was a second reason you wanted to be here when I woke up?' she reminded him softly.

Gregorio felt the frown lift from his brow. 'I believe you are suffering under a misapprehension in regard to something you overheard me say earlier.'

Lia's tension was immediate in the wariness of her expression. 'Oh…?'

He nodded. 'I am not…comfortable with emotions.'

She smiled ruefully. 'I noticed.'

'Let me finish, Lia,' he reproved gently. 'Sebastien was being his usual irritating younger brother self this morning.'

'Obviously I can't speak from personal experience, but I believe that's part of a sibling's job description.'

'Perhaps,' Gregorio allowed dryly. 'Sebastien seems to think it is, at least.' He sobered. 'What I said to him, about resolving the situation with Richardson so that you could return to your apartment, was not meant as literally as I believe you have taken it.'

She frowned her puzzlement. 'I don't understand...'

'Nor did I until I tried to find a reason why you were being so dismissive of me,' he admitted. 'Lia, *you* were the one who brought an end to our...relationship.'

'Our going to bed together, you mean? Well... Yes.' Her gaze didn't quite meet his. 'It was clouding the issue. Obviously, having known and liked my father, you feel some sort of responsibility towards me. But I assure you—'

'I feel *concern* for you, not responsibility.'

'Oh.'

He nodded. 'I realise some of my actions and comments may have come across that way to you, but I assure you that *responsibility* is the last thing I feel when I look at you or touch you.'

'Oh.'

'Now you are worrying me,' he drawled. 'The Lia Fairbanks I know always has plenty to say on any subject,' he explained as she frowned. 'Lia, has it occurred to you that I could just as easily mistake *your* responses to *me* as gratitude?'

Her eyes widened. 'You think I went to bed with you out of *gratitude*?'

He smiled slightly. 'What I think is that we should start being honest with each other, so that in future we avoid these misunderstandings.'

The only words Lia heard were *in future*. That implied the two of them were going to *have* a future. Maybe not as anything more than friends, but even friendship was better than *responsibility* or *gratitude*.

'I'm waiting for you to start being honest,' she prompted after several long seconds of silence.

Gregorio chuckled at her guardedness. 'I have been honest with you from the beginning. I told you when we met again last week that I'd wanted you from the first night I saw you in Mancini's with your father and Richardson.'

'And now you've had me.'

'Yes.'

'I… This is in the spirit of honesty, you understand?'

'I understand.'

'Well. I… You're only the second man I've… Well, that I've…'

His brows rose. 'I am only your second lover?'

'Yes.' Lia breathed a sigh of relief that she didn't actually have to say the words. 'And in comparison the first one was awful,' she said with feeling. 'Not that I'm comparing you to David in any way,' she added quickly. 'I just want you to know that our lovemaking was spectacular. Wonderful. Special.'

'In the spirit of honesty?'

She frowned up at him. 'Are you mocking me?'

'Not at all.' Gregorio chuckled. 'In the spirit of the same honesty, can I say that our lovemaking was— Lia…?' He prompted against the fingertips she had placed over his lips.

'I really don't want to hear how I measured up to the legion of women you've had in your bed.' She grimaced.

'I seem to recall that a Roman legion comprised about five thousand soldiers, and while I *have* been sexually active for some years, I very much doubt the total of my bed partners comes anywhere near that number.'

'You *are* mocking me!'

'Only a little,' Gregorio acknowledged huskily. 'And only because I am honoured to have been your second lover—especially as the first was such a failure.' His voice lowered. 'What I would *really* like above all things is to be your last lover too.'

'Sorry?' Lia's mouth had gone dry. Did Gregorio mean…? Was he asking…?

No, of course he wasn't. Gregorio didn't *do* for ever. She must have misunderstood him.

'Lia…' His hands moved up to cradle each side of her face as he looked down at her intently. 'Beautiful Lia. Our lovemaking was spectacular to me too. Wonderful. Most of all, special.'

'It was?' Lia wasn't sure she was still breathing. She couldn't possibly be awake.

'It was,' Gregorio confirmed gently. 'I wanted you from the moment I saw you, but in just a few days I have also fallen in love with you.'

Her eyes widened. 'You *love* me?'

'So very much.' Gregorio had only realised how much earlier, when he had contemplated the huge gap Lia would leave not only in his hotel suite but in his life, his heart, when the time came for her to leave and return to her own apartment.

Lia swallowed. 'Really?'

'Really,' he confirmed. 'Perhaps I always did. I have never believed in love at first sight, but...' He leant over to pull open a drawer in the bedside cabinet and remove something from inside. 'This is the handkerchief I used to wipe the blood from my cheek the day you slapped my face at the funeral.'

'You keep it in your bedside drawer?'

'Silvio gave it to me that day.' He smiled ruefully. 'I placed it in this drawer when I returned home, and it has been here beside me every night since.' He dropped the handkerchief back in the drawer. 'I couldn't bear to part with it.'

'You *love* me?'

'I do.' He nodded. 'More than life itself. Rather than wanting you to leave, as you believe, if I could I would keep you here with me for ever. But all of this is too soon for you.' He sighed. 'You lost your father such a short time ago. Your engagement ended badly. You need time to heal. To make a life for yourself. To prove to yourself that you *can* make a life for yourself.'

'You can understand that?'

His smile became warmer. 'You would not be the Lia I love if you did not feel that way.'

She looked up at him searchingly, noting the love and pride shining in his eyes as he steadily returned her gaze, leaving himself and his emotions wide open for her to see.

'Gregorio.' She reached up and touched his cheek. 'I've fallen in love with you, too.' She spoke clearly, firmly, wanting there to be no more misunderstandings between them. 'I love you,' she said. 'So very much.'

Gregorio felt as if someone had punched him in the chest, stealing all the breath from his lungs and rendering him incapable of speech. Lia *loved* him?

'How can you possibly…?' He was finally able to force words past his shock. 'You cannot possibly… You believed… You accused me of…'

'Yes. Yes. Yes. And yes,' Lia acknowledged emotionally. 'I did, and I believed all of those things. And *still* I fell in love with you. Because you're none of those things, Gregorio. You're honourable. Truthful. Protective. You have been nothing but kind to me even in the face of my less than gracious behaviour towards you. How could I *not* fall in love with you?'

'Dios mio…' Gregorio continued speaking in Spanish as he buried his face against her throat.

'I have no idea what you're saying, but I don't care because I'm sure it's something beautiful.' Lia laughed happily, her arm about his shoulders as she clung to him.

He lifted his head, his mouth now only inches

away from Lia's. 'I said you are beautiful. My heart. My world.'

'I love you, Gregorio. I love you so very much.'

She lifted her head and claimed his lips with her own.

'I said you would be bossy in bed,' Gregorio murmured indulgently a long time later, when the two of them were lying naked in bed together, Gregorio on his back, Lia nestled against his side with her head on his shoulder.

Their lovemaking had necessarily been gentle, because of the cast on Lia's arm, but no less beautiful because of it. Perhaps more so, because they had taken the time to explore and appreciate every inch of each other. Not just in passion and pleasure, but in love.

'Lia, when this is over there is a question I wish to ask you.'

Lia felt as if her heart had leapt into her throat. 'Why can't you ask me now?'

'For all the reasons I stated earlier.' He sighed.

'I want you to be sure—*very* sure—when you give me your answer.'

She frowned. 'And what happens in the meantime? Between us, I mean? Do we go our separate ways and meet up again in three months' time, say, to see if we both still feel the same way?'

'No!' Gregorio's arms tightened about her possessively. 'Absolutely not. We will see each other every day. And we will share the same bed every night,' he stated firmly.

Lia could barely hold back her smile of happiness.

Gregorio loved her. She loved him.

And whether Gregorio ever asked her that question or not was unimportant, because she had absolutely no doubt they would be spending the rest of their lives together.

EPILOGUE

Three months later

'YOU LOOK BEAUTIFUL,' Cathy said emotionally as she adjusted Lia's veil outside the church in her role as matron of honour.

Today was the happiest day of Lia's life. The day she and Gregorio were to be married.

She glanced down at the engagement ring she had transferred to her right hand for the duration of the ceremony. A solitaire yellow diamond, as Gregorio had said it would be. To Lia it was a symbol of their love and happiness together, and a promise for their future.

'Do stop fidgeting, Rick,' Cathy teased her husband as he stood beside Lia, ready to escort her inside the church and give her into Gregorio's safekeeping for the rest of their lives together.

'You look gorgeous,' she reassured him with a light kiss to his lips.

Lia found it hard to believe that this was happening. Six months ago she had thought her world was coming to an end—now she knew it was just beginning.

This was the first day of the rest of her life with Gregorio, as his wife.

'Ready?' Cathy prompted brightly.

'Oh, yes,' Lia confirmed without hesitation.

The last three months had been a rollercoaster of emotions. Gregorio's telling her he loved her. David's arrest and charges of embezzlement and fraud having been added to the charge of grievous bodily harm for his attack on Lia. Her days being occupied with making a success of her job at the Exemplar Hotel—which she had. And all her nights being spent in Gregorio's arms.

Throughout it all Gregorio had been the constant. Always there. And always, *always* assuring her of his deep love for her.

Today was their wedding day. A day when they would reaffirm their love for each other before family and friends.

She placed her hand on Rick's forearm before stepping forward, which was the signal for the two ushers to open the church doors and for 'The Wedding March' to be played.

And there, waiting for her at the altar, stood Gregorio, love and pride shining unreservedly in his eyes as he looked at her.

An unshakable love Lia knew she would return for the rest of her life.

* * * * *

If you enjoyed
AT THE RUTHLESS BILLIONAIRE'S
COMMAND
why not explore these other stories
by Carole Mortimer?

THE REDEMPTION OF DARIUS STERNE
THE TAMING OF XANDER STERNE
A BARGAIN WITH THE ENEMY
A PRIZE BEYOND JEWELS
A D'ANGELO LIKE NO OTHER

Available now!